ALWAYS THE GENTLEMAN

Longarm had heard enough. He took three long strides and his hand locked on the man's arm. "The lady is going to give you back your money, Mister. I think you better take it and leave—while you're still able."

Irma started to step between them. "Elliot is real fast with a gun. Custis, I don't want you killed!"

"You hear the lady?" Elliot asked. "She don't want you killed, which is what you are going to be unless you clear out fast."

"Touch that gun and I'll shove it down your throat," Longarm warned.

Elliot went for his gun . . .

TABOR EVANS

LONGARM

AND THE
SECRET ASSASSIN

JOVE BOOKS, NEW YORK

LONGARM AND THE SECRET ASSASSIN

A Jove Book / published by arrangement with
the author

PRINTING HISTORY
Jove edition / December 1996

All rights reserved.
Copyright © 1996 by Jove Publications, Inc.
This book may not be reproduced in whole
or in part, by mimeograph or any other means,
without permission. For information address:
The Berkley Publishing Group, 200 Madison Avenue,
New York, New York 10016.

The Putnam Berkley World Wide Web site address is
http://www.berkley.com/berkley

ISBN: 0-515-11982-2

A JOVE BOOK®
Jove Books are published by The Berkley Publishing Group,
200 Madison Avenue, New York, New York 10016.
JOVE and the "J" design are trademarks
belonging to Jove Publications, Inc.

PRINTED IN THE UNITED STATES OF AMERICA

10 9 8 7 6 5 4 3 2 1

LONGARM
AND THE
SECRET ASSASSIN

Chapter 1

U.S. Deputy Marshal Custis Long was quite mystified as he entered one of Denver's seediest saloons and waited for his eyes to adjust to the dim light. His boss, Billy Vail, had left a message saying that they needed to have a very private meeting, the sooner the better. Longarm could not imagine why they needed to meet in such a rough saloon as this instead of in the comfort and security of their huge Federal Building on the corner of Cherokee and Colfax Avenue.

The Bulldog Saloon was crowded and thick with smoke. The floor was covered with dirty sawdust, and as his eyes adjusted to the dimness, Longarm could see that there was a large and boisterous crowd gathered at the back bar. A few painted ladies were working the customers, and there were four or five poker and faro games in progress. The Bulldog had a notorious reputation, and Longarm knew that it generated nightly brawls and several murders each month.

Where *was* Billy?

"Hey!" Billy called from a tiny booth along the east wall of the room. "Over here!"

Longarm eased his way through the crowd and joined him. A huge bald and sweating waiter with shoulders like a bull and a neck as thick as Longarm's thigh brought them a pitcher of warm beer and two dirty glasses.

The waiter was a brutish-looking fellow missing the top half of his right ear and the index finger of his left hand. The prominent ridges over both eyes were thick with scar tissue, and his nose had been smashed flat, requiring its owner to do all his breathing through his mouth.

"A dollar," he grunted, holding out his meaty fist and sizing Longarm up with a clear challenge in his deep-set black eyes. "You ain't lookin' for no trouble, are ya?" he asked almost hopefully.

"Nope," Longarm assured the brute with mock seriousness. "We don't believe in violence."

The waiter stared at him, not sure if he was being conned or not. "But you ain't a peaceable-lookin' man."

"Oh, but I am!" Longarm exclaimed, sure that he was dealing with someone who had suffered brain damage. "And so is my friend."

"That's right!" Billy said, giving the hulking waiter a dollar and an extra ten-cent tip. "I assure you that all we want is to be left alone to drink our beer in peace."

"Okay," the brute said, giving each of them one last going-over before he shuffled away.

"I wonder what jungle or cave they found that one in," Billy said, filling their glasses.

"I don't know, but I'm pretty sure I once saw him

fighting in the ring. He used to take on all comers with one arm tied behind his back for a dollar a round, but few men lasted past the first."

"Even with one hand tied behind his back?"

"Yeah," Longarm said. "He could kick like a mule and break your skull with a single punch. He was almost mobbed when he bit off a local favorite's nose the night I saw him fight. A few days later, I heard that three men with clubs jumped into the ring and beat him half to death while the crowd cheered. I'd always wondered what happened to the man."

"Well," Billy said, "now you know. He serves beer and whiskey in a Denver piss-hole."

Longarm tasted his beer. "I remember thinking that the man could have earned a fortune if he'd been managed correctly."

"Listen," Billy said, leaning closer, "I didn't ask you to meet me so we could talk about a waiter. I've got a serious problem to discuss."

"So I guessed. But why couldn't we have talked it over at the office?"

Billy actually looked around as if someone might be eavesdropping before he leaned even closer and whispered, "Because it has to do with the department. We've got *big* internal troubles, Custis."

Longarm drew a five-cent cheroot out of his vest pocket and stuck it into the corner of his mouth. He folded his arms across his chest and said, "I'm listening."

"All right. As you very well know, the entire department has been in chaos since Commissioner John Pinter committed suicide."

"Sure," Longarm said. "Everyone in the department took Pinter's death real hard. Stupid and thoughtless

3

damned thing for him to do. Billy, what in the hell was the matter with the commissioner anyway? I never took him for a man that would kill himself. He had a fine family and—''

Billy leaned even closer and whispered, ''Maybe he *didn't* commit suicide.''

Longarm studied his boss. United States Marshal Billy Vail was a short, heavyset man who looked harmless but was not. He'd been a deputy marshal just like Longarm and a very good one, which was why he'd been promoted from the field to a desk job. Longarm liked and respected his immediate superior, and he knew that Billy was not one given to wild murder theories or twisted imaginings. If Billy believed that the evidence was starting to point toward the commissioner having been murdered rather than committing suicide, then this really was going to be a serious conversation.

Longarm removed his cheroot and emptied his beer glass. He poured another, giving himself time to recover from this shocking revelation while saying, ''One of our best men investigated Commissioner Pinter's death. He said Pinter had obviously been drunk when he jumped off the top of the Federal Building to his death.''

''Custis, what if our commissioner was *forced* to drink whiskey and then *thrown* to his death?''

''Who would do a thing like that?'' Longarm demanded. ''And off the top of our own building?''

''Good question. And the very same one that I have been asking myself ever since I spoke to Commissioner Pinter's widow. You see, she told me a few things that I never would have learned while the commissioner was alive.''

''Such as?''

Billy drained his own glass, then refilled it before he

continued. "Such as that Commissioner Pinter had a paid *secret assassin* hidden on our monthly payroll."

"No!"

"It's true," Billy vowed. "Mrs. Pinter couldn't name the man. She'd never even seen him, but knew that he did exist. Pinter actually called him. 'The Assassin.' "

"Did anyone else know about this?"

"Probably." Billy sighed. "I expect that the governor himself might have had knowledge of this individual. Maybe even a senator or assemblyman or two. But you can bet that none of them would admit the fact."

"What else could Mrs. Pinter tell you?"

"She said that her husband was very upset the last few days before he suddenly plunged to his death."

"Did she say why?"

"Mrs. Pinter thought it had something to do with the Marble Gang being allowed to post bail."

"I still can't understand that decision."

"Me neither. But what I suspect is that the commissioner botched the case. We also had the misfortune of getting a very lenient judge."

Longarm bristled. "It was a travesty of justice! That gang is clearly guilty of murder, extortion, and bank robbery."

"It gets worse—they all skipped town," Billy said. "And here's the *really* interesting part. Before they left, the Marble Gang torched a house over on Sixth Avenue. They were seen by neighbors running away after the fire started."

"Why would the gang start a fire?"

"That's what I want you to find out," Billy said. "From what little I've already discovered, the family that lived in this house consisted of a husband and wife and their young son."

"Did they all die in the fire?"

"They found the charred remains of the boy and his mother. The father either wasn't at home at the time, or else managed to escape with his life from the burning building."

Longarm pulled a pad and paper out of his pocket. He quickly scribbled down the address of the fire and said, "What was the family's name?"

"Smith. They were the James Smith family—though I'm sure that was just an alias. The neighbors knew almost nothing about them. They were very quiet and kept to themselves."

"What has all this to do with the Marble Gang?"

"I'm not sure," Billy said, "but think about it. They murdered this family and then immediately skipped town. That tells me that the Smith family had something very important to do with the case. And there's one other thing that you should know."

"I'm all ears," Longarm said.

"It's that the neighbors described Commissioner Pinter as a *frequent* late-night visitor to this house. Custis, are the same alarm bells starting to ring in your ears that are ringing in mine?"

"Yes," Longarm said. "Have you started the hunt for the Marble Gang?"

"Of course. Without any fanfare or publicity, we have launched an intensive hunt for those five men. But I don't expect to find them."

"Why not?"

"They had a small fortune of bank money hidden," Billy said. "So much that the damned prosecutor was trying to strike a deal for a reduced prison sentence in exchange for the recovery of that stolen cash. I fought hard to nix that deal. Those men are ruthless killers.

They'd have gone on another lawless spree the moment they were released."

"They're as bad as they come, all right. How'd the department finally pin the goods on them?"

"Now that is a very complex secret," Billy replied, "even to me. I suppose part of it would have come out during their trial, at which time I'm sure we'd have learned something more about our mysterious Mr. James Smith."

"The one you think is The Assassin."

"That's right."

Longarm frowned. "And of course, if he was responsible for their capture, then that would explain why they torched his house."

"Exactly!" Billy steepled his pudgy fingers. "If James Smith died in that fire—and we should know one way or the other any day now—then it will probably never be known if he really was The Assassin. But if he survived, the question is—what will he do now?"

"He'll go after the Marble Gang for revenge."

"I agree," Billy said. "He'll be relentless in hunting them down and killing them."

"Would that be so bad?"

"It would be contrary to every principle we hold dear concerning due process and justice."

"I guess it would."

"And The Assassin wouldn't just kill the gang members," Billy said. "He'd *torture* them—horribly."

"How do you know that?"

"We've discovered a few of his victims over the years," Billy said, taking another long pull on his beer. "You see, it's my theory that Commissioner Pinter only used this man on the rare occasions when it became obvious that we couldn't—for one reason or another—

obtain a murder conviction against a known killer. And so, rather than allow the killer to go free on some legal technicality, he'd hire The Assassin to mete out the justice.''

"Vigilante justice.''

"No, much worse than that,'' Billy assured him. "The Assassin's victims that we know about were all tortured before their deaths. Custis, this man *has* to be stopped!''

Longarm drank another glass of beer, trying to digest all that he'd just learned. Finally, he looked across at his grim-faced boss and said, "So you think that James Smith is The Assassin and that *he* forced Commissioner Pinter to drink whiskey and then threw him off the top of our building.''

"That's right. It makes perfectly good sense when you think about it. Smith, or whatever his real name is, risked his life and that of his family to bring in the Marble Gang. Soon afterward, Commissioner Pinter fails to seal the case down tight enough to keep a slick lawyer from convincing Judge Franklin Getty to grant the gang bail. Once on the loose again, they murder Smith's wife and kid in retaliation and try to make it look like an ordinary house fire.''

"But if all this is based on revenge, then why didn't Smith murder Judge Getty?''

"I think,'' Billy said, "that if The Assassin yet lives, that's *exactly* what he's going to do next.''

Longarm tossed down his beer and stood up to leave. In his haste he accidentally bumped into the brutish waiter, who was carrying another tray of beers, and they spilled all over the man and a table of customers.

"Uh-oh,'' Billy said as waiter whirled around with

his fists cocked. "Custis, I think you've just made a very, very unfortunate mistake."

Billy was right. Longarm could see the demented fury in the bruiser's eyes as he swayed forward.

"Now wait a minute!" Longarm said, throwing up his hands. "It was an accident. Honest!"

But the man wasn't listening. Instead, he lunged forward with an overhand that Longarm managed to duck and that actually penetrated the saloon's thin wooden wall. It took Longarm but an instant to decide that discretion was the better part of valor and to leap toward the nearest exit. And he'd have made it too if some sneaky bastard hadn't tripped him and sent him sprawling into the sawdust.

The waiter pulled his fist free of the wall, then roared as men scrambled out of his path. He would have kicked Longarm's head in if Billy hadn't made a flying tackle and knocked the brute off balance.

"You're on your own!" Billy shouted, scooting through the doorway as Longarm lurched to his feet and braced himself for another furious onslaught.

The enraged waiter scrambled up from the sawdust cursing and spitting. He swung again and Longarm ducked, but the professional fighter nailed him with a left uppercut that slammed Longarm into wall.

Longarm jabbed the waiter twice with hard, jolting punches that momentarily knocked the bruiser back on his heels and broke his nose, causing a torrent of gushing blood. The brute roared and came in swinging. Longarm, knowing that he could not trade blows with this demented monster, drew his six-gun and slammed it across the charging man's forehead.

The attacker's eyes crossed, and yet he still tried to grab and crush Longarm, who had little choice but to

9

pistol-whip him even harder. The man collapsed and Longarm staggered backward. The fellow who had tripped him the first time tried to do it again, and Longarm pistol-whipped him across the bridge of the nose, splitting it wide open and making him howl.

Longarm didn't wait around to see who else wanted to get up and fight. Instead, he dashed out the door just in time to see Billy Vail disappear up the street toward the Federal Building.

Chapter 2

Longarm followed Billy Vail into the Federal Building and went to his own department, where he had a desk, a chair, and a stack of files. He was not surprised to find an envelope marked CONFIDENTIAL on his desk. So Longarm sat down and opened the envelope. The top page inside contained Judge Franklin Getty's address, as well as that of the former Smith home. There was also a rough sketch of James Smith, although Longarm thought it too vague to be of much value.

At the bottom of the page, Billy had boldly printed: SECRET ASSASSIN. AGE, HEIGHT, WEIGHT, COLOR OF HAIR ALL UNKNOWN. NO PHOTOGRAPHS. EVERYTHING LOST IN FIRE. GOOD LUCK.

The second page contained several newspaper clippings with information on the Marble brothers and the other three members of their gang, including some suspected hideouts and the names of a few of their nearest relatives.

Longarm returned everything to the envelope and slipped it inside his coat pocket.

"Leaving already?" one of the other deputies asked.

"Yeah," Longarm said. "Got a new case."

"Where they sending you this time?"

"I don't know," he replied. "I guess I'll go wherever the trail leads me."

"Sounds mysterious," another man commented, curiosity stamped all over his face.

"I hope not," Longarm told them both as he left to walk down the hall to see Billy Vail.

He nodded to Henry, the clerk in Billy's outer office, and knocked on the open door to Billy's inner sanctum.

"Custis? Come in," Billy said from behind his big desk. "Close the door behind you."

When Longarm was settled in the chair across from Billy, the older man went on. "Take as much time as you need. Keep a tab on your expenses. Feel free to wire for as much money as it takes to wrap everything up neat and tidy."

"Do you mean really that?"

Billy nodded. "Just take care of everything and don't leave any loose ends that could come back and destroy a damned good department."

That last remark startled Longarm because Billy had never said such a thing before. But Longarm supposed it made sense. If the Marble Gang, led by Tom and Dave Marble, were captured alive, they'd probably tell everyone about The Assassin, and that could cause a major embarrassment.

Billy and his superiors right up to the top of the bureaucracy would, of course, claim that Commissioner Pinter had been the only one who had known about The Assassin. But the newspapers would smell the lie and it

12

would cause the department some bad publicity.

"And Custis?"

"What?"

Billy lowered his voice. "I am quite sure that you had better make Judge Getty your first order of business."

"I understand," Longarm replied, knowing that the man's life was in grave danger. It seemed very likely that James Smith, or whoever he was, would first seek revenge against the lenient Superior Court judge before setting out to kill the Marble brothers and their gang.

Longarm wasted no time after that. He had the judge's address, and trusted that he was not already too late to warn the man and perhaps save his life. Longarm knew Judge Getty very well, and held him in complete contempt. Getty was one of those fellows who had great knowledge of the intricacies of the law but possessed not a whit of good, practical sense. He couldn't see the forest for the trees, and was constantly allowing dangerous criminals back into society, often on the basis of some legal technicality.

Defense lawyers loved Judge Getty, and well they should, because he was almost always more sympathetic to the accused than to the victim. To Longarm's way of thinking, the softhearted and senile old judge should have been removed from the bench years ago. His lenience had cost the citizens a huge amount of heartache and grief. Still and all, Longarm realized that he had to protect the judge. The man might be softhearted and softheaded, but even his harshest critics agreed that Judge Getty's integrity was above reproach and that the old fool was incorruptible.

On his way out of the Federal Building, Longarm decided to make a quick detour over to Sixth Avenue in order to visit the burned remains of the Smith house.

Maybe he could find some useful evidence, or at least speak to one of the neighbors to learn if anyone had seen the arsonist. If he had a little more information, it might make convincing Judge Getty a lot easier. The man was notorious for being stubborn and closed-minded. And he was such an idealist that he might dismiss the possibility of a threat against his life unless Longarm had more to act upon than just a hunch that James Smith wanted revenge.

Ten minutes later, Longarm was standing in front of the remains of the Smith household. Apparently, it had been a rather large house with two brick fireplaces, both of which were still standing with a basement foundation. A very unhappy-looking policeman was shoveling through the ashes. The officer was very glad to stop his work and talk once Longarm showed his badge.

"What are you digging for?" Longarm asked.

"They still haven't been able to locate Mr. Smith's body," the dispirited sergeant replied. "They think he might have been trapped down in the basement when the fire started and we just haven't found his remains yet."

"I see." Longarm squatted on his heels. "But you *did* find the remains of Mrs. Smith and the boy."

"That's right. And we found evidence that a fire had been set. This wasn't any accident."

"What evidence did you find?"

"One of the investigators found an empty can that he said the arsonists used to hold kerosene. He showed it to me and said he could definitely identify the smell of kerosene, but I couldn't. Can you?"

"No," Longarm answered, "but I never did have an especially good sense of smell."

"Well," the policeman said, "this Detective Clark

claims he does have an excellent sense of smell. And he showed us how the fire started in the back of the house and then flowed up the walls, across the ceiling, and into the second story.''

''I see.''

''They can tell a lot about a fire,'' the policeman said, wiping his sooty brow. ''It was real interesting how he pointed it all out to us.''

''So there's no doubt that it was arson resulting in at least two murders.''

''Exactly. And that's why I'm still here digging and poking around. I can you this much, Marshal. Whoever lit the fire was one deranged sonofabitch.''

''Yeah, he'd have to be.''

The sergeant shook his head. ''I don't suppose you heard that the woman and her son had also been stabbed.''

''No!''

''They were. Both of 'em must have been murdered before the fire was set. The coroner found the blade marks on their rib cages and chest bones. It seems pretty likely that the fire was set just to wipe out the evidence of at least a double murder. Pretty cold-blooded, huh?''

Without answering, Longarm turned and began to walk very fast down Sixth Avenue, heading over to Tenth in order to reach Judge Getty as quickly as possible.

The judge lived in an impressive two-storied Victorian mansion a few blocks east of town near Washington Park. When Longarm bounded up onto the man's front porch, there was no sign that anyone was home. Longarm pounded hard on the massive door made of oak and adorned with squares of clear and stained glass.

"Judge Getty! Judge! It's United States Deputy Marshal Custis Long! Open up, please."

A middle-aged woman appeared at the door. She peered through one of the little glass panes and said, "Show me identification, please."

Longarm produced his badge and held it up for her inspection. Satisfied, she opened the door and smiled graciously. She was very attractive. Formally dressed and wearing a magnificent pearl necklace and earrings, she had soft, probing blue eyes, a slender figure, and a complexion that seemed to have never known, even for one hour, the direct ravages of the sun. "Excuse me for asking for your identification," she said. "Franklin has made a few enemies in his time. He just opens the door for anyone, but I'm a lot more suspicious."

"You're doing the right thing," Longarm assured the elegant woman. "Are you Mrs. Getty?"

"No, she died eleven years ago. I'm Franklin's sister-in-law, Lavinia. What can we do for you today, Marshal?"

"I'd like to see Judge Getty."

"He's taking his customary afternoon nap. Would you care to come inside and have tea while he sleeps a little longer? Then I'll awaken him and announce your presence."

"All right," Longarm said, following the woman into the parlor and taking a seat.

"Be right back," she promised. "Do you like sugar and cream in your tea?"

"A little sugar will be fine."

"One . . . or two lumps?"

"One, ma'am."

Lavinia returned ten minutes later carrying a silver tray and teapot, spoons, and china teacups and saucers.

16

Longarm let the woman prepare the tea, and then they sipped it quietly for a few moments before he said, "Have you lived with the judge a long time?"

"Since his wife died. He really does need someone to care for him. I'm afraid that Franklin is a trifle forgetful these days, you know."

"I suppose that eventually it happens to the best of us," Longarm said, wanting to appear understanding.

"You are a rather *large* man, aren't you," Lavinia said with surprising frankness. "And I'll bet you are a real tough customer too!"

Longarm blushed a little because of the sparkle in Lavinia's eyes and the bold way she was inspecting him.

She giggled and sipped more tea before adding, "Have you been a marshal for a long time, Mr. . . ."

"Long," he told her. "And yes, I have."

"Are you here on professional business?"

"I'm afraid that I am."

Lavinia's smile slipped. "What is the nature of your business—if you don't mind my asking."

Longarm carefully weighed his response. He had no intention of telling anyone—not even Judge Getty—about The Assassin and the role that he had secretly played for Commissioner John Pinter. However, Longarm did need to warn both the judge and his astute sister-in-law that they were in grave danger. That being the case, Longarm decided to be as truthful as he possibly could, but also a little evasive.

"There is someone who has a grudge against Judge Getty," he offered.

"I'm sure that a lot of people he has sentenced have 'grudges' against Franklin."

"Yes, but this one particular individual has to be considered mentally unstable and quite dangerous."

"Who is he?"

"I don't exactly know," Longarm said. "His name may be James Smith and I have a rough sketch to show you. But beyond that, he's sort of a mystery."

"Why would he be a 'mystery' to Franklin if he's sentenced him in court?" Lavinia asked.

Longarm cleared his throat. "It's not that he's actually sentenced this man, but that he might have been too lenient on this man's enemies, allowing them to post bail and then possibly retaliate."

"Retaliate? In what way and against whom?"

Longarm wished that this old woman wasn't so sharp. She was very good at pinning him in a corner and not letting him loose. Longarm felt quite sure that she would see right through him if he tried to lie or become too evasive.

"Miss Lavinia," he began. "I can't tell you everything because my immediate superior had ordered me not to divulge any more information about this case than is absolutely necessary."

"But you've just said that Franklin's life may be in danger! How can you withhold information that is vital to us after telling me that our lives are in peril?"

"Let me show you the sketch while I elaborate," he said, worried that Lavinia was getting very upset. "Here, look at this drawing."

"My," Lavinia said, "he is a handsome young fellow. Really, he doesn't appear dangerous at all."

"This is only a sketch," Longarm reminded her. "And I'm not even sure that it's a very good one. The important thing is to warn both you and the judge and perhaps talk you into leaving for a while."

"You mean, go hide someplace?" Lavinia asked, looking quite taken aback.

"Think of it as taking a short vacation," Longarm told the woman. "There must be places that you and the judge would like to visit for a while. And then when this whole business has passed over, you can come back rested and without anything to worry about."

"Lavinia, what is Marshal Long doing here!" Judge Getty said, appearing in the doorway wearing pajamas and a bathrobe. He appeared as cross and rumpled as one might expect from an old man when his regular afternoon nap had been interrupted.

"Judge Getty," Longarm said, coming to his feet and spilling his tea in his lap. "I'm sorry for this intrusion, but we have a problem."

"*You* have a problem," the judge said, glancing down at the deepening stain on Longarm's pants.

"I'll get a dishrag and we'll have you tidied up in no time," Lavinia said, hurrying into the kitchen.

"What are you doing here?" the judge demanded.

"We believe that your life is at risk," Longarm said, feeling the antagonism and mutual dislike rising up strong between them. "I've come to warn and protect you until the danger is past."

"What danger!" Getty scowled. "Marshal, what in blazes are you talking about!"

"The Marble Gang," Longarm said bluntly.

"I'm not worried about them! They skipped bail. I expect that they aren't even in Colorado." Getty scrubbed his face with both hands. "All right. All right. Perhaps I did err in allowing them to make bail, but it was an error on the side of humanity and they'd hardly have reason to want to kill me for such a benign mistake in judgment."

"Not them," Longarm said as Lavinia returned to the room and handed him a damp dishrag. Longarm used it

19

to vigorously scrub at the large, dark tea stain, making it look as if he'd pissed in his pants.

"Then who!" the judge demanded.

"We're not sure," Longarm said, dragging the sketch out again from the inside of his coat pocket. "Perhaps his name is James Smith and he looks like this."

Judge Franklin Getty studied the sketch, then, with a dismissive snort, handed it back to Longarm. "I've never heard of a Mr. James Smith or seen this young fellow. You've made a mistake again, Marshal! You people are always jumping to the wrong conclusions so that you can use the power of your office to oppress the poor and harass the innocent."

It was all that Longarm could do not to give the old fool a piece of his mind and tell him just how much damage his pudding-headed thinking had already done.

Instead, Longarm swallowed his temper and said, "We think that this man suffered at the hands of the Marble Gang and might blame *you* for allowing them to be free on bail, which they skipped."

Judge Getty's jaw dropped and he started to say something, but Lavinia stopped him, saying, "Franklin, we both need to listen to this handsome Marshal Long. I'm sure he has better things to do than to come over here and cause us needless alarm."

"Don't be too sure of that, Lavinia."

"Listen," Longarm said, growing impatient. "I suggested to Miss Lavinia that you and she might want to take a short holiday until this business is cleared up and we can be sure that your lives are no longer in danger."

"No!" the judge stormed. "We're not running away to hide. If there really is a danger—which I very much doubt—then it's your job to protect and serve us!"

"I'll try to do that, Judge, but . . ."

"No 'buts' about it, Marshal Long! You just go take a seat on the veranda and protect us all you want, but we're not going anywhere."

"Franklin!" Lavinia pleaded. "What would be so terrible about taking a train ride up to Cheyenne and visiting some of our old friends for a week or two? And that would free up Marshal Long to do other important work."

"Absolutely not," the judge replied.

Lavinia turned to Longarm and said pleasantly, "Another cup of tea, Marshal?"

"Thank you, Miss Lavinia. I believe that I will take it on the veranda."

A few minutes later, when Longarm was seated on the Victorian mansion's wide veranda trying to cool off a little, Lavinia appeared with his steaming cup of tea and a cup of her own.

"I'm sorry for his bad manners," she said, taking a seat beside him. "Franklin has always been absolutely unbearable when he's awakened from his afternoon nap. I should have insisted that you return later."

"I couldn't have done that."

"You mean that this Mr. Smith or whatever his name is could attack us at any time?"

"I'm afraid so," Longarm said, taking his tea. "You see, he probably does blame Judge Getty for the Marble Gang's getting away free. And he's just suffered a tragic loss."

"How tragic?"

"His wife and his small son," Longarm explained. "We think it very likely that the Marble Gang set fire to their house and killed them while Mr. Smith was gone."

21

Longarm heard the teacup dancing on its pretty little china saucer when Lavinia began to tremble. He was sorry that he was upsetting her, but she seemed to be the only one in this household with any sense at all.

Chapter 3

As evening approached, Longarm's stomach began to growl with hunger. Fortunately, Lavinia appeared with a tray of hot, delicious food.

"Here you are," she said, sitting down beside him in the gathering gloom. "Roast beef, mashed potatoes and gravy, vegetables, and more coffee."

"Miss Lavinia," he said, "you are a gem."

"I feel badly that you can't come inside and join us for supper," she told him. "But the judge really does have a strong dislike for officers of the law. He thinks that you are all a bunch of power-mongers."

"What?"

"He's seen some terrible abuses of power by government agencies and authorities," Lavinia elaborated.

"But he's also seen the worst side of a criminal's violent nature," Longarm argued. "What does he expect—that we handle murderers with the same respect that we give to good, hardworking, and honest citizens?''

''I think he actually does.''

Longarm picked up a silver knife and fork. ''Please forgive me for eating in front of you.''

''Oh, no, go right ahead. I like to watch a hungry man eat. The judge only picks at his food.''

Longarm dug into his meal with relish. ''It's excellent.''

''Thank you.''

''The thing is,'' Longarm said, chewing vigorously, ''criminals like those Marble brothers will almost always mistake respect and fair treatment for weakness. There are exceptions, but they are rare.''

''I hope that isn't true.''

''It *is* true, Lavinia. I've been chasing outlaws for a lot of years now and the moment that I start trusting and giving them the benefit of the doubt, I'm a dead man.''

''How sad!''

''Yes, but it's very true. With a petty thief or a drunk who raises a little hell on Saturdays, sure, you can straighten them out, but not hardened criminals. The only thing men like that understand is power, authority, and force.''

''This James Smith,'' Lavinia said, ''is he a hardened criminal?''

''I don't know. But he is hard and he's even been very cruel.''

Lavinia shuddered. ''Would he really . . .''

''Yes,'' Longarm said, ''he most certainly would. That's why I need to stay close, and I can't do it sitting out here in the open. Smith might already have seen me. I need to be hiding inside.''

"I'm quite sure that the judge would simply not allow you to stay inside."

"Lavinia," Longarm said, looking up into her pale blue eyes, "it's not just the judge's life that is in jeopardy. It's yours too! I can't walk away and let you be slaughtered by a maniac just because of the judge's blind foolishness."

She was quiet for a moment, then said, "You don't have much respect for him, do you?"

Longarm stopped chewing. "The judge?" He took a deep breath. Finally, he said, "No, I do not."

"Did you know that he once caused three innocent men to be hanged?"

"No."

"It's true," Lavinia swore. "They were accused of murdering a stagecoach driver. Franklin listened to the overwhelming evidence against them and then sentenced them to hang the next day. He was pressured by local officials who were in turn being pressured by the electorate. It seems that the incumbent officials were up for re-election and the outcome of the trial was important to their political futures. Anyway, Franklin bowed to the pressure, the three were hanged, and . . . a week later, the *real* murderer confessed."

Longarm laid down his knife and fork, then turned to study Lavinia. "So *that's* the reason he's always been so lenient in court?"

"Yes. He vowed that he would never, ever be made responsible for that kind of horrible mistake again."

"Okay," Longarm said finally, "that explains things, but it doesn't make them right. Maybe he did hang three innocent men back then, but . . ."

"There's no maybe about it, Marshal."

"But," Longarm persisted, "he's made even worse

mistakes by allowing guilty men to go free and murder again. So because he's tipped himself too far the other way out of a deep sense of guilt, a number of innocent people have become victims.''

Lavinia was becoming upset. She started to get up and leave, but Longarm gently closed his hand on her forearm, saying, ''I'm sorry. I didn't mean to upset you. And I *must* be allowed inside the house so that, if there is a danger, I can respond immediately.''

''All right,'' she said, ''I won't lock the front door. When the judge retires—and he does so at eight o'clock every night—you just sneak into the parlor, remove your boots, and stretch out on the couch, which makes into a nice bed. I'll even leave you a freshly laundered pair of pajamas.''

''That's not necessary.''

Lavinia gave him a patient smile. ''Marshal Long, I forbid you to sleep in your street clothes night after night.''

''All right, but . . .''

''You just wear the pajamas and I'll see that you have a pillow, a few blankets, and everything else that you need to be comfortable while you're on watch. And I fully expect you would hear anyone illegally breaking into our house on the ground floor.''

''I expect so,'' Longarm said. ''But in case I fall asleep, you have to promise me that you'll lock your door every night until this threat passes.''

''I promise.''

Longarm nodded with satisfaction. ''Lavinia, you're a fine cook and a wonderful companion for the judge. Please don't be angry at me for saying this, but you're better than he deserves.''

''That's not true,'' Lavinia said. ''He's a fine man.

You just don't understand him, even after I've confided his greatest personal tragedy.''

"We're supposed to learn from our mistakes," Longarm said doggedly. "Not make others suffer for them."

"Precisely," Lavinia said, excusing herself and going back inside.

Longarm finished his meal, and would have liked to have lit a cigar as darkness fell. But he dared not. The glowing tip of a burning cigar would be a red flag to James Smith if he was hiding somewhere out in the darkness waiting for his opportunity to murder the judge. No, Longarm thought, better to wait until the judge went to bed, then go inside, hole up on the couch, and wait through the night for a possible visitor.

Longarm certainly hoped that The Assassin came soon. Every day that he had to keep watch over this household was one more day that the Marble Gang had to put distance between themselves and Denver as well as to cover their tracks.

Precisely at eight o'clock, the upstairs light went out. Longarm remained in place for another hour, then slipped out of his chair and into the house. Tiptoeing into the parlor, he found a candle burning beside a tray holding a bottle of excellent brandy and a snifter. The pajamas were folded neatly beside the couch, and there were clean sheets, a pillow, and blankets.

"Lavinia," he mumbled, "you are too good to be true."

Longarm changed into the pajamas, and placed his six-gun beside the couch so that it was quick and easy to reach. He enjoyed two shots of the excellent brandy, and then climbed into his very comfortable couch bed. Just before drifting off to sleep, he heard the hallway grandfather clock strike ten.

27

"Darling?"

He awoke with a start, hand flashing for his six-gun.

"Darling, it's Lavinia."

She was sitting on the edge of the couch, and although he'd blown out the candle, there was enough moonlight in the parlor's windows to see that she had a glass of brandy in her hand and was leaning close.

"Is something wrong!" he whispered in alarm. "Did you hear someone outside?"

"No."

"Then what are you *doing* here?"

"I was worried that you might be uncomfortable. That the couch wasn't long enough."

"It's fine, if I bend my knees," he told her, relaxing.

"Would you like me to pour you another brandy?"

"No, but I would like you to go to bed."

Lavinia's lips turned into a pout. Longarm had a hunch that she had been sipping brandy since eight o'clock. That impression was strengthened when she placed her brandy down on the floor and reached under the covers to stroke his hard stomach.

"Lavinia," he asked, "are you *drunk*?"

"Yes," she admitted, "with desire."

"This is *crazy*! What if the judge came down here and caught you with me?"

She shrugged and her hand slipped down to his crotch. "Marshal, you know what a forgiving man Franklin is."

"Dammit, Lavinia," he said, feeling his manhood beginning to stiffen despite his concerns. "I don't think you know what you're doing."

"Oh, yes, I do," she said, stroking him harder, and then using her free hand to unbutton her own pajama top. "I have been waiting for a stroke of good fortune like this for a long, long time and I'm not about to pass up on the opportunity."

Before Longarm could form any more arguments, Lavinia was pulling aside his covers and climbing all over him. She was a wild woman and one too long denied. Lavinia mounted him and, for the next half hour, Longarm let her have as much fun as she wanted. At last, when she collapsed forward, moaning and shuddering, he kissed tears from her cheeks.

"It was worth the wait," she whispered in his ear. "And it's been a long, *long* wait."

"That's a pity," Longarm said, meaning it. "You're far too much a woman to be wasting your best years caring for that senile old codger upstairs."

"He used to come to my bed," she confessed. "For three years after my sister died, he came almost every night. I felt immense guilt, of course."

"Why?"

"Because I enjoy the act of sexual union so much. And I felt guilty because my poor sister was lying in a grave and I was lying in her husband's arms."

"You shouldn't have felt guilty. Do you feel guilty about this?"

"Heavens, no!" Lavinia exclaimed. "And I hope that James Smith takes his good sweet time in coming to exact his revenge. I want just as much of you as you can stand."

Longarm had to chuckle. "Lavinia, you are quite unlike any woman I've ever met. You're a real marvel."

"I was afraid that you would refuse me," she shyly confessed. "You know, because of my age."

"How old are you?"

"In my forties, but the juices are still flowing."

"I can tell. And," Longarm added, "I wasn't about

to turn you away. You're still a very desirable woman, Lavinia. You really should find yourself a man much younger and healthier than Judge Getty.''

''I couldn't leave him now when he needs me so very much.''

''Who said you had to leave him?''

''You mean, just invite big, handsome young studs like you over to make love to me in his parlor?''

Longarm had to laugh. Lavinia smiled and began to kiss his face, then his chest, and then . . . then he closed his eyes and let his physical sensations run wild.

Deep, deep into the night, Longarm awoke to find Lavinia gone. He started to drift back to sleep, but then he heard an upstairs window shatter followed by Lavinia screaming. Longarm snatched up his gun and lurched off the couch, bulling his way toward the sound of the shattering glass.

''Marshal!'' Lavinia screamed. ''Custis!''

Longarm plunged down the hallway, and then took the stairs to the top landing. His heart was already pounding, and he was sure that he'd slept through another assassination.

''Custis!''

''I'm coming!'' he shouted, running blindly down the hallway and finally reaching an open bedroom door where a candle flickered in a draft of wind.

''Oh, Custis!'' she cried, racing across the room to throw herself into his arms. ''He *hanged* Franklin!''

Longarm's blood went cold as he stared at the frail old body in pajamas slowly swinging from an immense chandelier that was half pulled out of the ceiling because of the unaccustomed weight of the judge's body.

Judge Franklin Getty's eyes bulged from his skull,

and his thin, white lips were stretched open wide in a silent scream as his body slowly swayed back and forth.

Longarm pushed the woman away for a moment and hurried to the shattered window. He stuck his head outside just in time to see the merest hint of a shadow floating down the back alley.

Longarm tried to raise the window, but it was stuck. It was clear that the murderer had sneaked inside either when he and Lavinia had made love or afterwards, when they had dozed off. The man had come upstairs, probably gagged and bound the judge, then hanged him, or rather, strangled him.

"Did you see anything?" Longarm asked, turning to face the shocked and trembling woman. "Anything at all?"

"Not very much," Lavinia breathed. "I awoke and left you to come upstairs a few minutes ago. That's when I heard . . . heard the gagging and strangling sounds. I thought the judge might be having trouble and I rushed inside, surprising the killer. He tried to open the window. I screamed. He jumped right through the glass and was gone. That's all I saw."

"Would you recognize him?"

Lavinia began to cry. Longarm hurried over and put his arms around the woman. "It's going to be all right. I'm sorry about the judge, but you're the one who is more important. And there is no reason for the killer to return again. None whatsoever."

"I saw a little of his face," she was finally able to whisper. "Not much, but a little."

"Did he look anything like the sketch I showed you?"

"No."

"Then what . . ."

"I could smell . . ."

"What!"

"Burned flesh."

Longarm hugged Lavinia even tighter. The horrible picture in his mind of James Smith's burned, flesh-seared face was enough to make anyone hysterical.

Chapter 4

Longarm wasn't looking forward to telling his boss, Billy Vail, about last night's assassination of Judge Getty. It was hard to admit that he had been sleeping downstairs on the judge's own couch when the gruesome hanging had taken place. He would not, of course, admit that he had earlier spent a few pleasantly exhausting hours with the sex-starved and very passionate Lavinia, making love and sipping the judge's excellent brandy.

"Come on in," Billy said, looking surprised and anxious. "And close the door."

Longarm closed the door and took a seat across from Billy. He fidgeted for a moment, and then decided to come right to the point. "The Assassin got to Judge Getty last night. I expect that you'll be hearing about it very soon. But I wanted to tell you what happened first."

"Damn!" Billy breathed. "I thought you were going straight to his house to look out for him!"

"I tried," Longarm said, "but he was very antagonistic. He accused me of being a 'power-monger' and refused to allow me to stay close to him.''

"So The Assassin found a way to do it, huh?''

"Yeah.''

When Longarm chose not to elaborate, Billy grew impatient. "All right, give me the details.''

"You aren't going to like this.''

"Tell me anyway,'' Billy snapped.

"The Assassin got into his upstairs room, gagged him so there wouldn't be much noise, then found a curtain cord and hoisted him up on a chandelier.''

"Oh, shit!'' Billy swore. "He *hanged* Judge Getty!''

"A proper hanging would have been a mercy,'' Longarm said. "The judge was hoisted up into the air like a flag on a pole. From the look on his face, I suspect that he had a relatively slow, horrible death.''

Billy groaned. "Wait until the newspaper reporters get ahold of this story. They'll have a wonderful time with it, and I don't have to tell you who will be blamed.''

"It was my fault,'' Longarm admitted. "I should have *insisted* that the judge allow me to sleep in an adjoining room. In fact, if it hadn't been for his housekeeper and companion, I'd have been sleeping on the porch instead of downstairs in the parlor.''

"Judge Getty was a sonofabitch,'' Billy said, leaning back in his office chair and lacing his fingers behind his head. "I'd be a hypocrite if I said that I wasn't secretly glad to be rid of the old softheaded fossil. No one deserves to be strangled to death, of course, but you can't blame yourself, Custis.''

"Oh?''

"Really,'' Billy insisted. "Nobody ever *insisted* that Judge Getty do anything. He was arrogant, stubborn, and

34

opinionated. And since there really was nothing that you could do, don't blame yourself. That's all that I'm saying."

"All right, I won't," Longarm replied. "But now I haven't a clue as to where to start looking for Commissioner Pinter's secret assassin—even if his name is James Smith, which I'm sure is just an alias."

"I quite agree," Billy said. "It seems that we have lost the trail. I don't suppose that you found any clues at the judge's house?"

"The judge's housekeeper and companion caught a glimpse of the killer."

"She did! Excellent, we can—"

"The woman told me that she smelled burned flesh."

Billy wasn't squeamish, but he did grow a shade paler at this news. "The woman was very fortunate not to have also been murdered."

"Yes," Longarm said. "The Assassin escaped through the window, then jumped off the roof and ran into an alley. After that, his tracks were lost on the street."

"Such a man should not be that difficult to find. Do you suspect he was burned in the fire that claimed his wife and son?"

"I do," Longarm said. "And now that he has exacted his savage revenge upon Judge Getty, I don't see any reason for him to remain here in Denver. Why should he?"

"No reason that I can think of."

Longarm came to his feet. "This secret assassin sure didn't waste any time moving against the judge, so I'm betting that he also won't waste any time going after the Marble Gang."

"That makes sense." Billy also came to his feet.

"Then I guess we both agree that, since we haven't a clue as to the whereabouts or identity of the assassin, you should go after the Marble Gang. If you find them before the vengeful James Smith, you can set a snare for him."

"Yeah," Longarm agreed. "But I'll tell you this much. I won't feel too badly if our assassin kills a few of that gang before I can trap him."

Billy frowned. He picked up a brier pipe and stuffed its carbon-coated bowl with Moroccan tobacco from a polished walnut case. His eyes narrowed and he stabbed the stem of his pipe at Longarm.

"Custis, it's your sworn *duty* to protect and serve the supposedly innocent until they are are tried and proven guilty. That even includes the likes of Dave and Tom Marble, as ruthless a pair of fugitives as I ever hope to see hanged."

"Speaking of them, what have we got to go on?"

"We believe that they've fled into the Rockies and are hiding in one of mining towns. Perhaps in Leadville, Cortez, or Durango. I don't think its inconceivable that they've split up and intend to regroup later at some pre-arranged location."

"I'll need every piece of information you can give me, not only on the Marble brothers, but on the other three members of the gang."

"Jake Mill, Hank Trabert, and Red Skoal. They're almost as bad as the Marbles," Billy said. "All three have spent time in federal prison. They're a bunch of misfits and murderers. They all should have hanged years ago, and would have been if it hadn't been for judges like the late Franklin Getty."

"Any of them married or have families?"

"One of them—Red Skoal—is from up around South

36

Park. Trabert is from Leadville, and I don't have any idea where Jake Mill is from, but he was once arrested over near Cortez.''

"What about the Marble brothers?''

"They were raised in Durango, but ran wild all over the Four Corners area,'' Billy said.

"That's damned rough country.''

"It doesn't get much rougher,'' Billy agreed.

"I'll need a top horse. Pack mule too. A good rifle and plenty of food and ammunition.''

"It's already been arranged,'' Billy told him. "You just go over to Johnson's Livery, where everything is waiting.''

"What about money?''

Billy's eyes narrowed. "How much do you think you'll need?''

"I have no idea.''

"You can always wire for more,'' Billy said, pulling out a drawer and handing Longarm a fat envelope. "This contains all the information we have on the Marble Gang as well as three hundred dollars in travel money. I want you to promise to wire me at least every other day so that I know what to tell *my* superiors about this case.''

"That's not going to be possible, Billy. There are no telegraph lines up there.''

"Figure out something,'' Billy snapped. "One of your glaring shortcomings is not to keep me informed when you are out in the field.''

Longarm opened the thick brown manila envelope and counted the money while saying, "I've heard you had exactly the same shortcoming when you were out in the field doing important work, Mr. Vail.''

Billy snorted, but when he saw that Longarm was smiling, he had to grin as well. "Just get over to that livery, get on that horse we've provided, and head for the hills, Custis. And remember that while you are tracking the Marble Gang, James Smith or whatever his name is might also be tracking *you*."

"I hadn't even thought about that," Longarm admitted. "I just assumed that The Assassin would be between me and the gang."

"That could be a fatal error in judgment," Billy told him. "Put yourself in Smith's place. If you didn't know where to find the Marble Gang, wouldn't you at least consider trailing a deputy United States marshal—one you probably already knew a great deal about because you'd secretly worked for this department?"

"I suppose that I might," Longarm agreed. "But I don't think that he can shadow me through the mountains."

"Maybe he's even smarter than we've given him credit for," Billy suggested.

Longarm folded the envelope in half and jammed it into his coat pocket. Turning on his boot heel, he started for the door, but Billy called out to say, "What was she like, Custis?"

He froze, not daring to turn for fear that his expression would betray him. "What do you mean?"

"The judge's housekeeper and *personal* companion. Just how *personal* was she?"

"Go to hell," Longarm growled as he continued out the doorway hearing Billy's laughter.

Longarm had promised Lavinia that he would stop by the judge's house and tell her what was going to happen next, and he was a man of his word. But first, he went to his own rooms and gathered his traveling bag and riding clothes, then his old canvas bedroll. He had several rifles of his own, but preferred to use the government's weapons so that, if they were damaged or stolen in the line of duty, he wouldn't have any personal losses. It took less than fifteen minutes for Longarm to pack what he needed and to hit the street again. Wearing a heavy sheep-lined leather jacket because he knew that the weather could get cold in October up in the Rockies, he headed for Johnson's Livery.

Bert Johnson had been supplying their department with good saddle horses for years. Like most deputies working out of Denver, Longarm did not own a horse. Therefore, the department found it more expedient and economical to rent rather than buy animals for its deputies, even when those animals were occasionally shot or stolen.

"Howdy, Bert!" Longarm said, dropping his belongings. "I understand that you've got an especially good horse and pack mule for me today."

"You got that right, fer damn sure!" Bert said with a wide grin. "Nothin' but the best for the best."

"You're a natural bullshitter if I ever heard one," Longarm told the grinning old-timer.

Bert was as sun-browned as Mexican leather and as wrinkled as rawhide. He had been a Montana cowboy for many years, but injuries had ended that way of life. So he'd come to visit Denver, been trapped into marriage by a bossy boardinghouse owner, and quickly escaped into the livery business. Longarm knew that Bert could have easily afforded to retire but that his wife was such a trial that he preferred to spend most of his waking hours at the stable.

"Which horse is it this time?" Longarm asked.

"He's a new horse," Bert replied. "Best of the lot. You'll be the first one to break him in right."

"I don't want to 'break in' a horse," Longarm told the livery owner. "I want Shorty, my usual horse."

"He's already rented out," Bert said. "So are most of the others you like. But this one is better'n all of 'em put together. His name is Target."

"Target! That's a hell of a bad name for a horse to be ridden by a lawman!"

"Well, then," Bert drawled, "call him Trigger or Goldie or whatever you want. He's a big palomino and he's strong, smart, and fast. He's got enough stamina to gallop over to California and back without breaking out into a sweat."

"The hell you say," Longarm growled.

"I mean it, Custis."

"All right then, let's see this wonder horse."

Bert led him to a stall, where Target was already saddled, saying, "I've even adjusted your stirrups and given you my best saddle and everything."

But Longarm wasn't listening. Rather, he was studying the palomino and, frankly, liking what he saw. The gelding was quite tall. He had a very intelligent, refined head and a deep chest, indicating good lungs and wind. Target was actually a deep golden color, if the poor interior light wasn't playing tricks on Longarm.

"Well," Bert said proudly, "what do you think?"

"He looks like a show horse to me," Longarm answered. "Why would you rent the government such a fine animal when you could sell him for a lot of money?"

"To be entirely honest, Marshal Long, the horse does have a few quirks."

"Quirks?"

"Yep. To begin with, Target can't stand dogs nor pigs nor chickens. He's not too partial to cats either."

Longarm folded his arms across his chest. "So what does he do about them?"

"He'll go after 'em."

Longarm took a moment to digest this information. "You're saying that he will *attack* pigs, chickens, and cats?"

"Afraid so," Bert said before quickly adding, "but a strong man like you can easily control Target with the high spade bit I'm putting in his mouth. You'll have no problems, Marshal, but a greenhorn or a lady . . . well, he's just too much horse for them kinda people."

"I don't know," Longarm hedged. "The last thing I need is a horse to worry about."

"Then *don't* worry about him! I rode this horse all over town yesterday."

"Then you must have seen at least one chicken or cat."

"Two," Bert admitted a little sheepishly, "and I can tell you that at least the cat got away alive."

Longarm ground his teeth. "What else do you have?"

"Nothing," Bert said quickly. "All my other sound horses are rented out right now."

"There are *other* liveries."

"Now Marshal Long! I tell you what. Because Target does need a little polish and training, I'll throw in the mule rent free. How's that for being fair?"

"Fair, hell! I don't care about what you charge the government for my pack mule! I just want steady, reliable transportation without any problems."

"And you'll have none! The mule never gave anybody a lick of trouble in his life. He's willin' and able. He'll be your friend and is better'n a watchdog because he hee-haws in the night if any strangers come around. In a pinch, you can also saddle and ride him."

41

"All right," Longarm relented. "I need to start traveling."

"How far are you going today?"

"I'll ride until sundown," Longarm told the man. "I hope to reach South Park tomorrow."

"Then you'd best be going now," Bert said, leading the saddled Target out of the stall and replacing his halter with the spade bit and a fine leather headstall. "You tighten the cinch and get mounted while I catch your mule."

"What's *his* name?"

"Geezer," Bert called back. "Or whatever you chose to call him given your spirit of the moment."

"Geezer will do," Longarm said, flipping up the left stirrup and then tightening the cinch.

Because he was going up into the Rockies, Longarm put some muscle to the cinch to make sure that it would not slip, stretch, or work loose on a steep trail. Target didn't like that one damned bit. The handsome palomino's ears flattened tight against his head and his neck snaked out. He snapped his big yellow teeth in warning, missing Longarm's shoulder by only a hair.

"Dammit!" Longarm cussed, backhanding the horse across its muzzle. "Don't you even think about biting me!"

Target pulled away suddenly, jerking Longarm completely off his feet. It took some doing to get the horse under control.

"Bert! I don't think this is going to work out between us this time."

"Oh, sure it will!" the old Montana cowboy cried as he dragged Geezer up and tied the mule's long lead rope around the saddlehorn. "You and Target just need to cover a few hard miles together. Right now, Target is just a little trail-rusty. Once you've worked the kinks out of him, he'll be as gentle as Geezer.''

Longarm wasn't happy, but he was in a big hurry. South Park was a long, long ride up into the mountains, and he'd be lucky to get within twenty miles of it before a veil of darkness dropped silently over the Rocky Mountains.

''If this horse gives me a bad time,'' Longarm warned, ''then . . .''

''Then sell him, buy a lesser animal, and we'll settle up the account when you return!'' Bert exclaimed. ''That's fair, ain't it?''

''Sure,'' Longarm growled, dropping his stirrup and mounting Target.

The palomino stood quietly. Geezer hee-hawed, looking forlorn and worried.

''Let's go,'' Longarm said, putting his heels to the palomino's ribs.

Target shot out through the livery's wide barn doors, and would have stampeded up the street except that he had to drag poor Geezer. The mule, slower, wiser, and very powerful in its own right, did not appreciate the severe pressure on its halter and began braying up the street, causing everyone to turn their heads, then grin at Longarm's discomfort.

''Dammit, anyway,'' Longarm swore, finally managing to rein in the headstrong palomino, ''this sure as hell is starting off all wrong.''

Chapter 5

Longarm made a quick stop at Judge Getty's mansion to say good-bye to Lavinia. There being no hitching post in front of the mansion, Longarm tied Target up to the white picket fence and kept the mule dallied to his saddlehorn. He could see that Lavinia had plenty of company, no doubt friends coming to extend their condolences. There were three or four carriages outside and a number of people milling around on the front veranda. Longarm could not see Lavinia and considered just leaving without a good-bye, but rejected that idea, knowing that it would be callous and break his promise.

When Longarm stepped onto the veranda, he was aware of how out of place he appeared among those who had come to pay the judge their final respects. To begin with, all of them were much older and more financially successful than he was. They were the cream of Denver society. Feeling entirely out of place, Longarm spied a maid carrying a tray of food and drinks. He snagged a glass of champagne.

"Custis!"

He turned to see Lavinia detach herself from a cluster of dignified men and come hurrying over to join him. She slipped her arm through his and steered him to the edge of the veranda. Tilting her head back, she said, "You know, you are by far the handsomest man here today."

"And by far the youngest," he replied, sipping his champagne. "I'm on my way out of town. I wanted to say good-bye."

Lavinia's smile faded. "Where are you going to start looking for that horrible murderer, or am I allowed to ask such a question?"

"Of course you can ask," Longarm replied. "Actually, now that James Smith has lost his family, we really don't have a clue as to where he can be found or know much of anything else about him. About the only thing that we can be sure of is that, now that he has murdered Judge Getty, he will direct his need for revenge against the Marble Gang. So, I'm going after them and I'll play the cards I'm dealt from that point on."

"Will he know your face?" Lavinia asked. "Will he know who you are and then try to kill you too?"

"Again," Longarm repeated, "I just don't have any answers. My job is to track the gang down, if necessary one by one. I can't say for certain, but I'm pretty sure that my path and that of our secret assassin will eventually cross."

"If he knows who you are and can recognize you, he'll have a great advantage."

"Yes, and I've thought of that. But Smith really was burned in the fire that took his family, and he's going

46

to be pretty easily remembered. I shouldn't have much difficulty picking him out of a crowd.''

Lavinia nodded in agreement. ''I don't suppose you have any idea when you'll return.''

''No.''

''Will you come back to visit me?''

''Of course. Will you be all right?''

''Judge Getty and my sister never had any children, and he left this mansion and everything else to me, including a very substantial bank account. I've nothing in respect to finances to ever worry about. In fact . . .''

She couldn't seem to finish so Longarm said, ''What?''

Lavinia took a deep breath. ''I know that I'm older than you and that we have very, very different backgrounds. But if you ever get tired of your hard and dangerous line of work, or get hurt, or . . .''

Longarm knew what she was trying to say, and he was touched. ''Thank you, Lavinia. You're a beautiful and passionate woman and you still will be forty years from now. But . . .''

''Is there someone else?''

''No,'' he said, ''it's not that at all. It's just that I don't think it would work between us and—''

''Shhh!'' she whispered, placing her fingers to his lips. ''Custis, please don't say anything more. You may change your mind some day. Let's just keep alive the possibility that I could give you sanctuary, love, and companionship—if you ever need me. All right?''

''All right,'' he said, leaning down to kiss the dear woman on the cheek. ''I'll be back and when I do, we won't have to make love on the parlor couch.''

Lavinia hurried away with blushing cheeks, and Longarm had started to finish his champagne when he heard a shout and then a scream. Suddenly, he turned to see his new horse, Target, tearing out fifteen feet of picket fence as the gelding tried to go after a yellow cat that had made the mistake of parading past the mansion.

"Target!" Longarm shouted as the cat disappeared under a hedge and the very distressed pack mule started to hee-haw.

Longarm vaulted over the veranda's railing, then sprinted across the judge's beautifully manicured front yard. Fortunately, Target was too encumbered to go very far since he was dragging the fence and a very upset-looking Geezer.

"Damn you!" Longarm swore, grabbing the palomino's reins and finally managing to untie them from the uprooted length of picket fence. "I'm not sure that you and I are going to get very far before I put a damned bullet in your stupid head!"

Target rolled his eyes, still looking for the yellow cat. People were crowded against the veranda railing staring at Longarm, the mule, and the handsome palomino. Longarm swung into his saddle and spotted Lavinia among the spectators. He wanted to tell her he was terribly sorry and embarrassed for tearing down what was now *her* nice picket fence. But instead, he just decided to wave good-bye. To his relief, she blew him a kiss, and he guessed it meant she really wasn't all that upset about the ruined picket fence.

He was angry at Target, and pushed the horse hard into the mountains. As promised, the palomino didn't even break out in a sweat. Target was in superb condition and showed no sign of fatigue, even after many hours of climbing. Geezer, on the other hand, was very unhappy. And although the mule was lightly burdened carrying just Longarm's food, extra clothes, ammunition, and supplies, he was not nearly so youthful or energetic as Target and resented the difficult climb up into the Rocky Mountains.

Longarm rode until well after dark, and stopped at a little way station called Pine Flats where he'd gotten a room and meals on a number ot occasions. He paid the owner extra to put Target and Geezer in a stall instead of out in the corral with a bunch of other animals.

"You got any cats, pigs, or chickens on the place?" Longarm asked the man.

"Why, sure!"

"Well, this palomino doesn't like them," Longarm told the proprietor, Doug Paulson. "That's why he's much better off in a high-sided stall."

"What kind of horse is that?"

"He's got his peculiarities," Longarm said, "but he's a travelin' sonofabitch. I've never rode a horse that possessed such extraordinary stamina."

"Must have gotten it chasing other animals," Paulson opinioned. "Don't worry about him tonight. Come on inside and get a good feed and rest your bones."

"Thanks," Longarm said. "And remember that I prefer not to have folks know that I'm a federal marshal."

"Why is that?"

"It just gives me a little advantage, and you never know who might carry a murderous grudge against a lawman."

"Yeah," Paulson said, "I can see your point. Used to be people respected the law and those who enforced it. But these days, what with all the riffraff we've gotten coming into these mountains looking to strike it rich, no one knows who to trust anymore. Damn shame what things are coming to."

"Isn't that the truth," Longarm said, removing his hat and going inside to wash up and then to eat.

There were six other travelers who had decided to put up there for the night, and when Longarm sat down at the community table, they all nodded silently and went right on with the important work of filling their empty stomachs. Longarm did the same. Doug Paulson, the owner of this establishment, employed a grinning Chinese cook who served nothing but beef, potatoes, stewed tomatoes, and beans, along with the best sourdough bread for hundreds of miles around and cherry pies that would make any man come back for seconds.

Longarm wasn't disappointed in the meal, and afterward he dragged his chair over to a big rock fireplace. Feeling full and content, he lit a cheroot and smoked it in contented silence while the other guests chatted about the weather and the latest news concerning ore strikes and the general state of the world. Eventually, the subject of Judge Getty's murder came up as a topic of conversation.

"I heard from a stagecoach driver that someone murdered Judge Franklin Getty, that old sonofabitch who was always letting criminals off with just a slap on the wrist," a large, whiskered freighter remarked to no one in particular.

"Whoever killed that judge ought to be given a damn medal!" another guest opined. "I hear tell that judge was taking money under the table from the accused and that's why he was letting them off so easy. I also heard that he had a pretty woman living with him in a big mansion and that he owned half a city block in downtown Denver."

"Then he *must* have been crooked as a damn dog's hind leg," another snorted. "Damned judges got way too much power, you ask me. Same as anyone that works for the damned federal government.''

Longarm saw Paulson wink, but managed to keep his silence. It was not unusual to hear complaints about the federal government, and Longarm had long ago stopped trying to defend his badge, his profession, and his employer. Besides, he had a very important assignment— to track down and arrest or even kill, if absolutely necessary, the members of the Marble Gang—and he was not a man who allowed himself to be easily diverted. At the same time, he would not duck trouble or turn his head when he saw the law being broken or abused.

Longarm smoked quietly, letting the conversation ebb and flow around him. Most of these men were rough miners and freighters with whom he held little in common. Gradually, the conversation began to die out and men started to get up and head off to one of the bunks that Paulson rented in a separate, community cabin for only fifty cents a night. Private rooms were a dollar, but Longarm figured they were well worth the extra price, especially when the ''damned government'' was picking up the tab.

He was about to leave when one of the men yawned and said, ''Glad that scar-faced sonofabitch that was here last night left. He was one scary bastard.''

Longarm froze in mid-stride. ''Excuse me,'' he said, ''did you say that a scar-faced man was here?''

''Yeah! You could see where he'd been burned like toast. He smelled like liniment too.''

Longarm looked to Paulson. ''What else can you tell me about this man?''

''Not much,'' Paulson replied. ''Why the interest?''

''I might know him. Did he give you a name?''

''Nope, and I didn't ask. He was a rough-looking customer but he had enough money for a private room. He just ate by himself without saying anything to any of us. Then he went to bed and was gone this morning.''

''Any idea where?''

''No.''

''What kind of a horse was he riding?''

''Bay gelding. Nice-looking horse but nothing real special. Certainly not as nice as that palomino you're riding.''

''Can you remember anything else about him?'' Longarm persisted, eyes swiveling from one man to the other. ''Anything at all.''

''Why, is he in trouble?'' the boarder asked.

''What makes you think that?''

''You just seem mighty interested in him all of a sudden, that's all.''

''He might be the same man who used to work for the people *I* work for,'' Longarm said, purposefully vague. ''I'd heard that he was in a fire and burned pretty bad. Thought maybe I could cheer him up a little, that's all.''

''He looked like the kind of a man that could use plenty of cheering up,'' Paulson said. ''He looked . . . angry. That's what he looked like.''

''How big is he?'' Longarm asked.

''Hey,'' the boarder said, ''I thought you said you worked together. What the hell is *your* story anyway?''

Longarm could see that the man was becoming belligerent. Taking a step back, he reached into his coat pocket and showed his marshal's badge. ''I'm a United States deputy marshal.''

Instead of getting angry or becoming abusive, the boarder threw up his hands and retreated a few steps. ''I don't want no more trouble with the law, mister! I mean it! I've been doing honest work since I got out of the federal pen almost three years ago. And Mr. Paulson can tell you that I been driving a wagon for the—''

''Whoa,'' Longarm said, putting his badge back into his pocket. ''I'm not interested in arresting or even questioning you about your personal business. I just need to know a few things about the man with the burns that you saw here.''

''That's all?''

''Yeah. Anything else you can tell me?''

''He was heavily armed,'' the boarder said. ''And he had a lot of cash.''

''How do you know that?''

''I saw that he was wearing two side arms, and what looked like a derringer was bulging up his left sleeve,'' the man told Longarm. ''As for the money, Mr. Paulson told me that he had a pocket full of double eagles and a wallet full of greenbacks.''

''That right?'' Longarm asked the owner.

''Yeah, he was loaded with guns and cash,'' Paulson answered. ''What did he do, rob a bank and try to torch it?''

''No,'' Longarm replied. ''We think he might have been the man that murdered Judge Getty.''

''But I hear Getty was hanged, not burned.''

''It's a long story that I can't disclose,'' Longarm told the two curious men. ''But if you see that man again, you need to immediately alert the federal authorities. The suspect is probably going to murder a lot more men if he isn't apprehended as soon as possible.''

''Well, I'll do that,'' the boarder vowed. ''I see that ugly jasper, I'll arrest him myself—if the feds have posted a reward.''

''They haven't,'' Longarm said, ''and I would

strongly advise you not to brace him under *any* circumstances.''

"He's a real killer, huh?"

"He is," Longarm agreed. "About as bad as you'll ever find. That's why I need to know if he said anything about where he was going next.''

"I'm afraid not," Paulson said with a frown. "But come to think of it, I did happen to notice that there was a lot of dew on the meadow grass this morning.''

"Meaning?"

"Meaning I could see that a horseman had ridden out and he was heading southwest, in the general direction of Leadville.''

"Thanks," Longarm told both men, "I appreciate the help and the information.''

"No trouble at all, Marshal," the boarder said, looking very relieved. "Always happy to be of assistance to the law.''

Longarm managed not to laugh out loud before he turned on his heel and went up to enjoy a good night's sleep.

Chapter 6

"Howdy," The Assassin said when he reined up in front of the open-doored blacksmith's shop and peered inside the dim recesses. "Can you please tell me where I can find a man named Hank Trabert? I understand that he hails from these parts and I've ridden quite a distance to find him."

The blacksmith, a thick, taciturn man, was laboring at his forge. His attention was riveted on the orange-colored horseshoe he was beating into shape across the horn of his anvil. And though the air was cold, his front shirt was unbuttoned almost to his waist and stained dark with perspiration.

Not bothering to look up at the polite stranger sitting astride the bay gelding, he growled, "Stranger, can't you see I'm busy? You want information, go ask someone that ain't got anything better to do. Don't bother me, dammit!"

Jim Smith's black eyes tightened at the corners with

anger as he watched the blacksmith shaping the horseshoe. The man was about his weight, but short and probably more powerful. After a moment of consideration, Smith dismounted and led his horse over to a tie rail. He tied the bay, then loosened his cinch, eyes locked on the unsuspecting blacksmith. Smith's hat was pulled down low. He wore a blue scarf that rode up high around on his neck so that the angry, crimson-colored flesh that lined his jaw was concealed. His black hair was now very long and shaggy so that no one could see the unpleasant remains of his left ear. With the bandages gone and a thick smear of grime and mud to cover a few other fleshy discolorations, The Assassin didn't attract all that much attention.

He still moved with the fluid grace of a big cat. His fingers, once nimble enough to handle a deck of cards with the skill of a professional dealer, were now covered with angry red scar tissue, but encased in soft doeskin gloves. Smith didn't care because he could still handle a gun or a rifle far better than most.

Smith surveyed the town, idly considering how much of a lesson in civility he would need to administer to the blacksmith. Had the fellow been simply indifferent, his manners could have been excused. But instead, this man had been rude and unkind. He had also been insulting, and Smith could not tolerate such treatment. This blacksmith lacked any sensitivity and had no concept of the real meaning of physical pain. He'd probably never lost a wife and a child or known agonies of the mind. He was a brute begging for a hard lesson.

Smith strolled into the blacksmith's shop. They were alone. No one would interfere. Still, as Smith watched the unsuspecting blacksmith, something inside demanded he give the man one last chance.

"I said that I'd ridden a very long way and that I really must find Hank Trabert. I used the word 'please.'"

The blacksmith swung around, hammer clenched menacingly in his fist. "And I told you to go to hell! I got work to do here and—"

The blacksmith never finished his sentence because Smith seized his wrist with both hands and shoved the man's hammer and fist into the fire. The blacksmith screamed and his eyes bugged out. He struggled in agony as the handle of his hammer and the flesh of his fingers seared and smoked.

"Ahhhh!"

Smith felt the fire heating the doeskin leather of his gloves. His lips drew back from his teeth and his scarred face pressed close to the blacksmith, who was trying to break free. Smith held the blacksmith's hand a moment longer against the coals of the forge, and then released him when the wooden handle caught fire.

The blacksmith collapsed to his knees, his left hand holding his right wrist. His face was suddenly very pale and his entire body shook as he stared at his blistered fingers.

Smith squatted down beside the man, their faces just inches apart. When he spoke to the whimpering blacksmith, his voice was gentle, almost compassionate. "I once read that being burned to death is the most painful way of all to die. I believe that, and I expect that now you do too."

"Get away from me!" the blacksmith screeched.

"You really are a very, very stupid man," Smith said, taking a handful of the blacksmith's hair and then slamming his face twice into the anvil, smashing cheekbones and nose to mushy pulp.

The blacksmith momentarily lost consciousness.

57

Smith stood up and looked around. He saw a can of rust-colored water that the blacksmith used to cool the iron hot off his forge. Smith picked up the can and poured it over the unconscious man's head until the blacksmith roused again.

Kneeling beside the whimpering man, whose face was now a mask of blood, Smith said, "Now, will you finally be kind enough to tell me where I can find Hank Trabert? Or . . . or do you need some more persuasion?"

The blacksmith's eyes widened with terror. "No!" he cried, rolling away from the forge and scuttling up against a wall. "He lives about four miles east of town. There's a big lightning-scorched pine by the side of the road. You'll see a wagon track heading off the left. They got a little spread up against the cliffs."

"How many folks are living there?"

"I don't know. Just the old man and a couple of his sons. Hank is the oldest and meanest, but . . ."

"Thank you," Smith said, rising to slap dust from his knees. "See how easy this all would have been if you'd only been courteous and polite at the beginning of our little conversation?"

The blacksmith managed to nod, but cried, "Mister, you're *crazy*!"

"No," Smith said, stepping back into sunlight. "But I have suffered deeply and believe everyone who is rude and coarse needs a good lesson in pain and humility."

He smiled at the trembling figure. "I think you have learned something here. I think that you will be kinder and more helpful in the future to strangers. Won't you?"

"Yes! But . . . but my hand! I can't work like this!"

"You'll find a way," Smith promised. "Believe me, the human spirit has amazing power and you *will* find a way."

58

The Assassin strolled back over to his horse and looked around. Leadville had grown since he'd last ridden though about five years ago. Clearly, the mining town was prospering. Why, they'd even built that magnificent structure called the Tabor Opera House just across the street! Perhaps when his mission was all over and every last member of the Marble Gang was dead, he would return to Leadville.

Jim Smith untied his horse. Looking up and down the street, he was about to mount and ride east as a tough-looking young cowboy rode up beside him to dismount and tie his own bay gelding.

"Good afternoon," The Assassin said pleasantly. "Nice day, isn't it."

The cowboy started to walk past without comment, but The Assassin's fist snaked out to seize his right forearm. Leaning in close so that their eyes were separated by mere inches, The Assassin, "I said *good afternoon*. Now, you need to say something like, 'Yes it is, and have a nice day.'"

The cowboy attempted to pull free, but The Assassin held him as if he were locked in a vise. The cowboy felt cold fear flood through his guts as he gazed into a pair of cold, dead eyes. There was also something very terrifying about this man's face. The cowboy gulped and managed to say, "Yes, sir, it sure is! And I wish you a nice day!"

"Excellent!" Smith said, breaking into a painful smile and releasing the cowboy. He then mounted his horse and rode away, pleased that he did not have to administer a second painful but important lesson in good manners.

* * *

Jim Smith had no difficulty finding the lightning-scorched pine and the road leading up to the Trabert place. It wasn't much of a place really, just an old cabin, a small, sod-covered barn and root cellar, and some busted-up wagons littering the yard. The only things of value were the four horses in the rickety pole corral and a spooky old milk cow tethered to a long rope—and she'd be worthless except to the Indians for butchering.

"Hello the cabin!" Smith called as he approached to within a hundred yards.

"Who goes there!" an old man shouted, emerging with a shotgun cradled across the crook of his left arm.

"I'm a friend of Hank's!"

"Who you be?"

"Smith! James Smith. Hank and I rode with the Marble brothers. Have you seen them lately?"

"Nope. Ride on up, stranger."

Smith rode up to the cabin, eyes shifting around to see if the old man was alone or if there was someone covering him from inside the cabin.

"Hank around?" he asked with a smile.

"No," the old man replied.

"Sorry to hear that," Longarm said, looking pained. "Who are you?"

"I'm Hank's pa. Name is Luke."

"Where did Hank go?"

"He and Ben went off early this morning to get some cattle. Said they'd be back before dark. I expect they will 'cause neither one of 'em can cook worth a damn."

"I'd be obliged if I could buy something to eat myself," Smith said, dismounting.

"What the hell happened to the lower part of your damned face?" Luke asked, making a face. "You get some kind of rash or something?"

60

"Yeah," Smith replied. "Mind if I tie my horse and come inside to eat?"

"As long as you got money."

"I do."

"Then come inside and fill your gut. I got some damn good chili cookin'."

"Much obliged."

Smith tied his horse, then loosened its cinch. He could feel the old man's eyes boring into him, but he pretended not to notice.

"You known my son Hank and the Marble boys long?" the old man asked.

"Naw," Smith said, patting his horse. "Just long enough to do a few jobs. I'm hopin' that we can do a few more and not get caught this time."

"Be a good idea," Luke agreed. "Come inside. Besides the chili, I've a pan of warm biscuits on the stove."

"Sounds good."

Smith followed the old man into the cabin. It was a rat's nest. Most everything was scattered on the floor including a lot of dirty, stinking underwear. One look around and Smith damned near lost his appetite.

"Just step over to the table and lay a dollar on 'er," Luke Trabert said, "before I fill your plate."

Smith didn't reach for his money. He wasn't about to pay.

"What did you say your name was again?" Luke said.

"Smith. James Smith."

The old man was filthy and dressed in bib overalls. He had a limp and droopy left eyelid, caused, no doubt, by a rather unsightly knife scar that ran from his left ear across his eye and then up into his scalp, where it disappeared in his silver hair.

"I make good chili and biscuits," Luke said as he used an enormous spoon to fill Smith's plate. "You'll like the taste of 'em but I can't guarantee that you'll like the way they will fire up your innards."

Smith figured that the old man was making a joke, so he chuckled.

"Here you go. Eat your fill. There's plenty more where those came from . . . hey, where's your dollar?"

Jim smith smiled. "Dammit, I guess I forgot to bring my money inside."

Trabert's expression changed. He grabbed up the plate and carried it over to lay it on his hot stove. "Get your gawddamn money or get your ugly ass outa my cabin!"

"Now, that's no way to be hospitable."

Luke shook his big, silver-topped head. "I ain't too sure about you, stranger. Hank never said anything about a James Smith riding with the Marble Gang. And I damn sure have a feeling that you didn't forget your money."

"No," The Assassin said, reaching for the gun at his side and drawing it from his holster to aim at the old man's chest, "but you sure as hell forgot your good manners."

When Luke lunged for his shotgun, The Assassin shot him in the side. The old man cried out and fell hard. He began to crawl toward the shotgun, and Smith shot him in the hand when he reached for it.

"No! No more!" Luke cried.

"Say *please*."

"Please!"

"I'm afraid that you're a little too late," Smith said as he put a bullet in the old man's head.

Smith stepped over the body and picked up the plate of chili. He forked some into his mouth and was prepared to spit it out in a hurry, but it was actually very good. He grabbed up a biscuit, and it was delicious.

"Damn," he said to himself, "that old man really could cook."

Taking his food outside, Smith squatted on his heels and began to eat. He was famished and there was plenty of food. His intentions were to eat it all before the Trabert boys returned.

Chapter 7

Jim Smith finished off the chili and biscuits, then tied his horse around behind the cabin. Daylight was fading fast and he was beginning to wonder if Hank Trabert and his brother Ben really were planning to return for supper.

Smith went back into the cabin and grabbed the old man by the wrists, then dragged his body back outside. The bay gelding, smelling death, grew agitated, and Smith had to drag the body a long ways out in the woods.

"Rest in peace, you old badger," Smith said. "I wonder how many good men you cheated, stole from, or ambushed in your worthless lifetime. One thing that's for certain, the world will be better off for your passing."

Smith went back into the cabin. He straightened it up, but did not bother to try to eliminate the large bloodstain. Instead, he found a burlap feed sack and draped it over the stain like a rug. Satisfied, he lit a lamp and began to search the Trabert cabin looking for anything of value. There wasn't much, but then he hadn't expected much. He did discover a nice little .45-caliber, two-shot derringer. It was a quality weapon with real pearl-handle grips, and Smith figured that the family must have killed and then robbed a gambler.

There were cash and coins hidden in a cracked teapot that added up to less than twenty dollars. Smith poured the money into another feed sack along with a few cans of peaches and a sack of coffee. He debated taking an old shotgun, but decided against it because the weapon had the initials LT carved into its stock. Smith knew better than to take anything that could be positively identified with this soon-to-be-deceased family of thieves and murderers.

There was a tin of good tobacco and the makings, so Smith rolled a cigarette and walked out into the trees, where he leaned up against a rock and smoked with contentment as he watched the sun melt into the western horizon. He heard a coyote howl, and a half hour later saw the dark silhouette of a great horned owl launch itself from a pine tree to swoop across the yard and then disappear on its nightly hunt.

Smith was a patient man. He had come to believe that patience was an extremely important quality in the killing game. Impatient men generally made foolish mistakes. And in the many cases where he had been hired as an assassin, Smith had come to realize that the first person who made a move was almost always the first to die.

Better, far better, to sit and wait like a cat ready to pounce on a mouse. By patiently waiting, a man chose his *own* moment of attack as well as the setting, and he also gained the critical element of surprise. And when he had his quarry at his mercy, it was good to remain patient and then to kill slowly.

Smith heard the whinny of a horse break the night's gentle peace, then the bawling of weary cattle. He snubbed out his third cigarette and stretched, not bothering to come to his feet. Out of the gloom he saw the silhouettes of cattle? And he heard the sound of voices. It would be Hank and Ben Trabert returning from some lawlessness. They would be very tired and hungry, while he was well fed and rested. That would be to his great advantage. Should he go into the cabin and greet them, or allow them to go inside and then discover the bloodstains under the burlap sack? Once that happened, they would come rushing outside, shouting for their dead father. And Smith would be waiting to gun them down in the lamplight now spilling from the cabin.

He played out the showdown in his mind using both scenarios while the brothers penned their stolen cattle. He decided it would be more interesting and possibly even safer to wait inside the cabin. Hank and Ben would not be expecting trouble and they would be easy to catch off guard. He would then feed them bullets instead of their father's chili beans.

Smith came to his feet, stretched, and then kept to the shadows until he reached the corner of the cabin. There would be a moment of danger, when he had to duck through the brightly illuminated doorway, so he paused and stared out toward the pens where Hank and Ben were finishing up their work. He could hear them talking and knew that they were well occupied. Taking a deep breath, Smith ducked low and slipped back into the cabin. He glanced all around and decided to use the darkest corner of the room for his ambush position.

Turning the wick of the lantern down ever so slowly, he grabbed a chair and went to that corner to wait, rather like a spider waiting in its web.

He did not have long to wait. The Trabert brothers came stomping across the yard. Their boots sounded on the front doorsill and they pushed inside.

"Pa?" one of the brothers called. "Where . . ."

"Which one are you?" Smith asked softly.

Both brothers swung around to face him, squinting and grabbing for their weapons. Smith drilled the larger of the pair in the belly, slamming him into the smaller one, who shouted in alarm and managed to get off a stray bullet. Smith took careful aim and shot the smaller man in the head, causing him to drop like a rock.

"So," Smith said, slowly easing out of his chair to stand over the bigger one, who was writhing about in agony, "which one are you? Ben . . . or Hank?"

The man looked up and cursed. He was holding his leaking stomach with one hand while the fingers of his other hand were stretching for his gun. Smith waited until those fingers brushed the gun, and then he stomped them with the heel of his boot, mashing the finger bones like dry twigs.

"Ahhhh!" the man screeched, tearing his hand away. "You sonofabitch! Who are you?"

Smith picked up the dying man's gun. It was worth at least ten dollars in any pawnshop. He stuffed it in his pocket, turned, and went to retrieve his chair as he listened to the big man moan and thrash about. Returning with the chair, he sat down on it backward so that he could rest his chin on his forearms.

"I'll ask you once more," Smith said, noting the gray pallor that was already beginning to etch its way across the man's stricken face. "Are you Hank . . . or Ben?"

"Hank!" the big man screamed, trying to focus. He was sweating profusely, still looking for a weapon.

"Good," Smith answered, quite pleased that the right man was going to suffer.

"I killed your father," Smith said matter-of-factly. "But quick, like your brother Ben."

"Who *are* you!" Hank screeched, raising his broken hand to shakily touch his pale, perspiring face.

"My name is James Smith."

Hank choked and his eyes dilated with terror. "You're The Assassin!"

"I've been called that," Smith said mildly.

"I should have known."

Smith came to his feet. He kicked the chair over and then squatted on his heels, just out of Hank's reach. "If you had only tried to kill me instead of my family, I would now put you out of your misery. But you and the others chose to burn down my house and murder my wife and son."

Smith began to shake with uncontrollable rage. "A beautiful woman and boy who never hurt anyone!"

"Shoot me!" the man whimpered.

"No," Smith hissed, lips drawn back from his teeth. "Too easy. Way too easy!"

"Please!"

But Smith shook his head, stood up, and took several deep, steadying breaths. "Does it hurt bad?"

"Kill me!" Hank Trabert pleaded.

"Tell me about the Marble Gang. Tell me *all* about them and then maybe I'll put you out of your misery."

Trabert gasped, "All right. Just tell me what you want to know!"

"Names. I think I have them all, but I want to be very sure. I wouldn't have killed your father and brother if

69

I'd had any other way." Smith sat down again. "You see, Hank, I'm not like you and the Marble brothers."

"You're worse!" Hank sobbed, looking down at the bullet hole in his gut. "You're *enjoying* this!"

"Maybe a little," Smith conceded. "Give me names and where I can find the others."

"Red Skoal has a little spread over in South Park. He's . . . he's the closest one."

"Does he live alone?"

"He lives with a Ute woman."

"What's her name?"

"I don't know."

"Go on."

"Jake lives in Cortez. When he's not riding with the gang, he's a saddle maker."

"Single or married?"

"Married! He's even got kids, dammit. Are you gonna shoot them down too?"

"Of course not. That's *your* style, not mine. Now, what about the Marble brothers?"

"I never been to their place."

"Where is it?"

"Arizona. Right . . . right in the corner."

"In a town or on a ranch?"

Hank threw his eyes about and moaned. "Kill me, please. I'm suffering!"

"House or ranch?"

"I don't know," Hank whimpered. "Ranch, I think. They . . . they move around a lot. You must know that."

"Anyone else responsible for the deaths of my wife and son?" Smith asked, his voice almost pleasant.

"No!"

Smith climbed to his feet and looked around the room.

"This cabin is a shit-house," he said more to himself than the dying man. "It stinks."

Hank began to drag himself across the rough plank floor, leaving a wide, crimson trail of blood. Smith waited until he reached the door, then walked over and grabbed Hank's boots and dragged him back across the room.

The man began to cry.

"All right," Smith finally told him. "I guess that you've suffered enough. Not as much as I have since you and your friends murdered my *innocent* family, but enough."

Hank was almost gone. He managed to raise his head. "Are you gonna shoot me? I hurt *so* bad!"

"No," Smith said, reaching into his pocket for a match. "I'm going to set this place on fire and let you burn when you go to hell."

"No!" Hank screamed. "No!"

But Smith paid the dying man no attention. He went over and grabbed the kerosene lamp, then hurled it to the floor. Some of the fuel splashed over Hank, who once again began to crab toward the door, cursing and wheezing.

Smith lit a match, pitched it onto the wet floor, and whirled for the door feeling the sudden and intense heat and hearing Hank's tortured screams. He slammed the door and propped it shut with a broken board.

He went out to the corral and calmed the nervous livestock. Night turned almost to day as the flames grew higher and higher. Fortunately, the cabin was in a clearing so that there was little danger of setting the forest afire, unless one of the rising embers landed in some dry brush.

Smith didn't think that very likely. He smoked one

71

more cigarette, then spread his blankets under the stars by the corral and watched the cabin burn and slowly collapse into a smoking funeral pyre. Smith supposed it might be a good idea to drag the old man's body over and throw it into the embers so that it would burn as well, but the idea was so distasteful that he rejected it and eventually fell asleep.

The sun was well up on the eastern horizon when he awoke the following morning. The cabin was a pile of smoking rubble. Smith was hungry and used hot coals from the cabin fire to cook a big breakfast. Afterward, he saddled his horse and prepared to ride on over to South Park, where he would find Red Skoal and his Ute woman.

He had heard a lot about Red Skoal and knew that the man was far smarter and more dangerous than the Trabert family. Smith also realized that he would have to be wary of the Ute woman too. Indian women had a strong loyalty for their men and they weren't squeamish or slow to kill.

Yes, Smith thought as he rode away with the taste of smoke heavy in the crisp morning air, *I might have to kill the squaw too.*

Chapter 8

Target threw a shoe and went lame about ten miles east of Leadville. Cussing over his bad luck, Longarm walked the palomino into a bustling mining town named Jasper Rock and immediately began to search for a blacksmith who could solve his problem.

"All right," he wearily said to himself, spying a blacksmith's shop. "I'll see if we can get Target shod and then find us a place to rest tonight. But tomorrow, I'm on my way to Leadville come hell or high water."

The blacksmith watched as Longarm slowly led his fine but limping palomino up the busy street careful to avoid being run down by the heavy flow of wagon traffic. When Longarm came to a stop and nodded a tired greeting, the blacksmith laid down his hammer and frowned.

"Looks like you got a big problem, mister. What'd that handsome palomino horse do, bow a tendon?"

"He tossed a shoe about four miles out on that rocky

wagon track you folks call a road. I'm hoping that he'll be sound once you tack on a new shoe and we give him a night's rest.''

"We'll see about that," the blacksmith said, wiping his rough hands on his leather apron before coming over to gently run his hand down Target's leg.

"My name is Joe Wheeler."

"Custis Long."

"Might take a little more time for this horse to get over his lameness."

"I hope not," Longarm replied, "because I can't wait. And despite a few personality problems, this is the toughest animal I've ever ridden. He never tires."

"This horse has a rock bruise," the blacksmith said after examining the hoof carefully. "Look here. You can see the dark spot where the blood has collected just under the surface of the foot. It's as nasty a bruise as I've seen in a good long while."

"Damn! I guess that means that I may have to leave him."

"You're in a big hurry, huh?"

"I am," Longarm answered. "What do you suggest?"

Joe moved around the horse, inspecting each hoof. Finally, he straightened and said, "This horse needs a day or two to heal and he needs new shoes all the way around. You can see that for yourself."

"Yeah," Longarm said, "I can. I was just hoping . . ."

"Hoping don't cut it in this rocky country. I'm sorry, but it just doesn't. He needs new shoes."

"What about the rock bruise?"

"If you weren't in a hurry, I'd suggest you stay off

74

this animal for at least a week. Then, I'd shoe him on all fours and I think you'd be just fine."

"Like I said, I can't do that."

"All right," Joe replied, wiping perspiration from his face with the back of his sleeve, "then I'll shoe him all around but do some special work on the bad one."

"What kind of 'special work'?"

"I'll make the shoe a little thicker and put a leather patch and padding over that rock bruise, then run a narrow crossbar from side to side for even more protection."

"That ought to do the trick."

"I'll make no promises. But tomorrow morning, we'll know if he's sound again or not."

"And there's nothing else that can be done?"

"Nope. The only other thing I can suggest is to sell this horse and buy another. But given your hurried circumstances, you'd really get skinned."

"I can well imagine," Longarm said, toeing the dirt as he weighed this unexpected dilemma.

"It's your choice to make," Joe said. "I'm a good shoer, third generation, and you won't find any better. But like I said, I can't make any promises, and the work that I'll have to do will take a fair amount of time."

Longarm appreciated the blacksmith's frank and honest assessment of the situation. "Tell you what, Joe," he said, "go ahead and make that special shoe for Target and we'll just hope for the best tomorrow morning."

"Target? That's his name?"

"Yeah, but I didn't give it to him, someone else did."

"Bad name. Maybe bad luck."

"How much for your work and board for both animals tonight?"

"I'll shoe the palomino all around for seven dollars

and I'll have to charge you another dollar each for boarding, which includes a heavy dose of oats.''

"Fair enough," Longarm said, digging money out of his pockets. "Can you also recommend a good cafe where a hungry man can get his money's worth?"

"Boomer's Cafe is the local favorite. It's just up the street."

"What about a clean hotel where a man can sleep without a bunch of hollering and fighting going on in the next room?"

"Frontier Hotel is the one you want. Nice and clean. They got a little saloon downstairs and a few gambling tables. But nothin' noisy."

"Thanks," Longarm said, paying the young blacksmith and then retrieving his rifle and saddlebags. "And by the way, the mule's name is Geezer."

"Now, that is a name that I *do* like," Joe said with a grin. "And I'll do the best that I can with that rock bruise. Before I build that special shoe, I'll soak his hoof in warm salt water to draw out the poison. That usually helps, if he'll stand for it."

"He will if he doesn't spy a cat, pig, or chicken."

"Huh?"

"Never mind," Longarm said, heading off and calling back over his shoulder. "I'll come around the first thing tomorrow morning."

"How much would you want to sell him for if he's still lame?" the blacksmith shouted.

"He won't be!"

Longarm went directly to the Frontier Hotel and rented a room for the night. The establishment was a little more raucous than Joe had described, but the upstairs rooms were clean and the doors were fitted with heavy sliding bolts.

"You'll have no trouble with anyone here," the hotel's proprietor vowed. "Unless you invite 'em in as your guest. Which brings me to a question."

"What's that?" Longarm asked, frowning at the man.

"Sir, are you married?"

"No."

"Then maybe you'd like a woman sent up. We have some girls that—"

"No, thanks," Longarm said abruptly. "I've had a long, miserable day and all I want is food and maybe a whiskey or two before I turn in early."

"I understand," the proprietor said. "And I respect your need for privacy, but our girls really are—"

"*Not* interested," Longarm snapped.

The proprietor gave him a curt nod and backed out of the room fast. Longarm bolted his door, then collapsed on his bed for a few minutes. He closed his eyes and must have dozed off because, when he looked around again, it was dark outside and his stomach was staging a full riot.

He lit the bedside lamp and washed his face in a porcelain basin. There was a fresh bar of soap and clean towels laid neatly on his bedside table, along with a note stating that a hot bath could be ordered for only one dollar. Longarm thought that might be a pretty good deal because he was gritty with a heavy accumulation of trail dust. He would have ordered the bath first and then eaten if he had not been so famished.

Boomer's Cafe was just down the street, and it was obviously the town's most popular eating establishment. Longarm had to wait a few minutes before he was able to get a stool at the long counter and order a steak with fried potatoes, sourdough bread, and apple pie for dessert.

"What will you have to drink, mister?" the heavyset and hustling counterman asked. "We got whiskey, beer, coffee, and even water."

"I'll have whiskey and water," Longarm said. "It's been a long day."

"You do look sort of bushed," the man said, showing Longarm a grin that was missing both front teeth. "So how do you like your steak?"

"Medium rare sounds about right."

"That's the way I like it myself," the man said, hurrying away to return a moment later with a shot of whiskey and a glass of water.

Longarm downed the whiskey neat, then signaled for a refill. He sipped the second and when his supper finally arrived, he attacked it like a starving wolf. The steak was two inches thick and delicious, not a bit tough. The potatoes were good too. Longarm ordered coffee with his apple pie, and was more than satisfied.

"You get enough to eat?" the man behind the counter asked, refilling his coffee for the third time.

"More than enough," Longarm said, paying his bill and starting for the door.

"You comin' back for breakfast?"

"I expect so," Longarm replied as he passed outside.

Longarm wasn't paying attention to where he was going and had no excuse when he plowed into a couple on the busy boardwalk.

"Excuse me!" Longarm said, grabbing the young woman. "I am sorry!"

She straightened herself and looked up into his face. A big smile creased her lips and she exclaimed, "Custis! Custis Long! My gosh, but it's been a while since I saw you last!"

"Irma?"

"Why, sure!" she squealed, throwing her arms around his neck and hugging him tight. "Who else! And how could either of us *ever* forget that wild night we spent together in Denver?"

Longarm grinned. "I sure haven't," he said, remembering that Irma was one of the wildest women he'd ever had in bed. Not only that, but she was pretty and amusing. They'd had one hell of a good time together.

"Come on, dammit," the man beside Irma growled as he yanked her roughly forward.

"Hey!" she cried. "Don't be so rough!"

"Yeah, well I didn't pay you three dollars to bat your eyelashes trying to drum up more business."

Irma tried to pull away, but the man jerked her even harder. "You want your money or not?" he shouted.

"You can have it back!"

"I don't want it back! Now come along or I'll—"

Longarm had heard enough. He took three long strides and his hand locked on the man's arm. "The lady is going to give you back your money, mister. I think you'd better take it and leave—while you're still able."

The man glared at him. He was smaller than Longarm and probably a little younger, lean and angry-looking. The man's hand dropped to hover over the gun resting on his hip. "Stranger," he growled, "I *paid* for this whore and I'm takin' her to my room. Now, if you want to see another sunrise, you'd best get outa my way."

Irma started to step between them, but Longarm eased her aside saying, "I think you'd better let me handle him."

"Elliot is real fast with a gun. Custis, I don't want you killed!"

"You hear the lady?" Elliot asked. "She don't want

79

you killed, which is what you are going to be unless you clear out fast.''

"Touch that gun and I'll shove it down your throat," Longarm warned.

Elliot went for his gun and he was fast. Longarm just had an instant in which to slam a straight right fist into Elliot's jaw, causing him to fire his gun into the board-walk. Before he could lift and take aim for a second shot, Longarm hit him with a vicious uppercut that sent him crashing off the boardwalk into an empty water trough.

When Elliot recovered enough to lift his gun in one last attempt to shoot, Longarm booted him in the crotch.

"Ahhhh!" the man howled, falling back into the empty trough and clutching his groin.

Longarm wrenched Elliot's pistol from his grasp and hurled it end over end so that it landed on the roof of the nearest building.

"You big sonofabitch!" Elliot screamed. "I *paid* for her.''

"Here!" Irma snapped, tearing Elliot's three dollars out of her handbag and hurling it into his pain-contorted face. "Keep your money! With your balls kicked half-way up your damn throat, I expect that it'll be weeks before you'll even be able to piss straight, much less pleasure yourself or some poor damn woman.''

Irma slipped her arm through Longarm's as people from a nearby saloon began to emerge, curious as to what all the commotion was about.

"My room or yours?" Longarm asked.

"Let's try mine first," she said, leading him away.

Her room was not as nice as his own, but it would do. She led him inside and then locked the door, saying,

"I've got some whiskey and I expect we both need a drink."

"I expect so," Longarm agreed. "Irma, I thought you were going to quit whoring."

"I will, one of these days."

"And one of these days some hothead like Elliot might kill you."

"I know," she said, finding a bottle and glasses. "Elliot is a bad one, all right. But he pays well and he never got rough with me before."

Longarm knew it was pointless to give this pretty young woman a lecture. Irma was her own person and as tough as nails. She was a brunette with a full figure and a mischievous smile that bordered on making her look slightly devilish. She also had gorgeous legs and a beautiful bottom. But tonight, he could see that she looked worn and world-weary.

Irma was trembling too, and Longarm pretended not to notice how the bottle rattled against the rim of their glasses as she poured their drinks.

"You haven't been taking care of yourself like you were in Denver," he said. "Why did you leave to come up to a boom town like this?"

"They ran me out of Denver." Irma handed him a whiskey. "Maybe I should have told the Denver law that you were my very good friend, huh?" she said.

She was teasing him and he knew it. "I very much doubt that would have cut you any slack," he replied. "But you could have come to my place and holed up until things blew over."

"I would have," Irma said, "but I made a mistake."

"What do you mean?"

"Well," she said, taking a big drink and sighing with regret, "I met a man in Denver who had struck gold up

81

here. He was doing the town and we got along pretty well. He had a damn feed bag of gold to spend, and I figured that he needed someone to help him celebrate.''

''I'll bet.''

''He was even nice,'' Irma said. ''I tried to talk him into a share of his gold mine.''

''Good for you.''

''He resisted . . . at first. But you know that I can be pretty persuasive.''

''I do know,'' he said, eyes dropping to the lovely swell of her bosom.

''His name was Darin and he begged me to come up here and stay in Jasper Rock with him.''

''And you agreed.''

''Why, sure! He owned a big gold mine. But before I agreed to come, I got him drunk, screwed his brains out, and made him sign an agreement giving me a third of his gold mine. After that, I figured I was finally on my way to riches.''

''Why is it,'' Longarm asked, ''that I have a feeling this story is not going to turn out well?''

''Because you're looking at a practicing whore. A very tired one too.''

''What happened to your mining man?''

Irma drained her glass. She poured a refill, then replied, ''Darin was shot to death the first night we arrived in this town. The next day, four different men showed up at the courthouse with false titles to his gold mine. My title was just a scrap of paper with his drunken scrawl.''

''And you were left out in the cold.''

''Almost.''

''You should return to Denver.''

But Irma shook her head. ''There's a lot of money to

be made in Jasper Rock. I intend to find myself another rich miner. I wish you were rich instead of just strong and handsome, Custis.''

''Sorry.''

''Don't be,'' she whispered, hands reaching for the buttons of his pants. She extracted his rod and rubbed it against herself until Longarm grew hard. ''Big as ever, honey.''

Longarm just smiled and sipped her good whiskey while she went to her knees and took him into her mouth. He closed his eyes and smiled with contentment.

''And you're as good as ever, Irma.''

After several minutes, he took her to bed and they eagerly made love. They were both tired and not quite as lively as they'd been down in Denver, but neither of them complained.

After Irma stiffened in ecstasy and then hugged his neck tightly, she whispered, ''Why don't you take me down to Denver and make me an honest woman? I'd be a good wife for you, even a mother if you wanted children.''

''Of course you would be,'' he whispered in her ear. ''But I'm not a marrying man. And besides, you must have figured that I was here on business.''

''Yeah, business,'' she said with a hint of sadness. ''Killing business, most likely.''

''I have to leave first thing tomorrow morning,'' Longarm told her. ''And I have a mule you can ride back down to Denver. Maybe a lame horse too. Anyway, when you get there, you'll have a key to my rooms. Why don't you just rest for a week or two until I return?''

''What if you *don't* return this time?''

''I will,'' he promised. ''I always do.''

''All right,'' she whispered. ''Whatever you say.''

She fell asleep in his arms. He would give her some money to live on. Irma was a good woman. She just needed a little breathing room and a change of attitude. Maybe he could help with that too.

They made love the next morning, and then Longarm tried to say good-bye without hurting her feelings. "I've just *got* to get moving, Irma. I'm on the trail of a man that I think is going to kill someone in Leadville."

"Maybe that someone needs killing."

"He does," Longarm said. "The man who's going to be killed is named Hank Trabert and he's a bad one. But I still have to try and save his life. That's my job."

Irma wormed the rest of the story from Longarm, and then she said, "Aren't you going to buy me breakfast?"

"Sure," he said. "But first, you'll have to accompany me to the blacksmith's shop. I had to walk into town last night because my horse went lame."

"I hope he *stays* lame," Irma said. "That way, you won't be off so soon to Leadville."

"Yeah I will," Longarm said. "Come on, honey. Get up and get dressed."

She stretched languidly. "Must I?"

Longarm had a very powerful urge to jump back into bed one more time with Irma before leaving. For a long moment, he weighed pleasure against responsibility, and pleasure won.

"All right," he said, "I'll have *you* for breakfast."

"I thought you might," she said coyly.

Chapter 9

"Well," Longarm asked, "how is Target this morning?"

"He's better," the blacksmith replied, "but he's still lame."

Longarm frowned while Irma said, "Pleased to make your acquaintance."

Joe blushed. "I've seen you around, miss."

"Irma. Everyone just calls me Irma. And so, if you've seen me around, then why didn't you come over to say hello?"

"I dunno." Joe cleared his throat nervously. "I'm . . . I'm generally short of cash."

Irma smiled. "As cute as you are, I might have been willing to work out a sizable discount."

Joe blushed so deeply that Longarm felt sorry for the young blacksmith. "Irma, give him a break. Joe, what do you suggest about Target?"

"That palomino needs a few more days of rest and

he'll be sound again. I can rustle you up a replacement mount, but it'll cost plenty. How far are you planning to ride?''

"Quite a long ways. Over to Cortez and the Durango area and maybe far beyond. It all depends.''

"Is your mule rideable?'' Joe asked.

"He's supposed to be.''

Joe nodded. "Then perhaps you should ride him and lead the palomino for the next couple of days. Not having to carry your weight would make it a lot easier on that rock bruise and might allow it to heal a little quicker.''

Longarm thought that this wasn't a bad suggestion, but he was in such a damn big hurry. Lives depended on him reaching the members of the Marble Gang before they were ambushed or executed by The Assassin. And Geezer, while he was a steady and willing enough mule, was slow. Longarm had been thinking of leaving the mule behind anyway.

"Tell you what,'' he answered. "Irma, as I recall, you're a pretty good horsewoman.''

"I am,'' she said proudly.

"So why don't you stay here a few days while Target's rock bruise heals, then have Joe saddle up Geezer for you to ride to Denver. You can jockey the palomino back there and wait for my return.''

"Sure, I can do that,'' Irma said. "You'll just need to give me a key to your place and tell me where to deliver the horse and the mule.''

"Okay,'' Longarm said, relieved to have a workable solution, "that's what we'll do—providing Joe here doesn't try to skin me too bad on a replacement mount.''

"I'll make sure of that,'' Irma said, stepping in close to the young blacksmith and slipping an arm around his waist. "You wouldn't want to make a little trade, would you, honey?"

He stuttered, then blurted out, "Miss Irma, you mean trade a piece of you for a horse?"

"A little loving for a very good, very *cheap* horse for my friend."

Joe gulped. He couldn't keep his eyes off the swell of Irma's breasts and his chin began to wag up and down. He appeared ready to drool.

"Yeah, Miss Irma, I think we can work out something that will make everyone *real* happy!"

"I thought maybe we could," she said, wrinkling her nose and batting her eyelashes.

Longarm felt a moment's passing annoyance. He was a mite jealous, but then reminded himself that Irma was just being Irma. Maybe she'd never change, even if some man did marry her and give her the respectability she needed so badly. Longarm didn't know, and right now he didn't particularly care. With Irma's help, he'd get a good replacement horse at a reasonable price. In addition, he would be done with Target and his quirks and free of the truculent mule as well. It seemed to him that everything was about to work out just fine.

"I better show you what I have in the way of good horses to loan," Joe said. "Come on back to my corral."

Irma beamed with triumph, but Longarm chose not to respond. Instead, he followed Joe back to a corral, where there were seven or eight horses, most of them sorry-looking.

"What do you think?" Joe asked. "Every one of them is well shod and sound."

"I'm not too impressed," Longarm said bluntly. "I

don't see a single horse in your corral that looks as if it could shake its own thin shadow.''

"What do you mean?"

"These look to me to be Ute Indian ponies. Scrubs." Longarm turned away, saying, "I'm on a manhunt, Joe. I *have* to be well mounted. My life and those of some others might well depend on it.''

"All right, all right!" Joe overtook him. "You can use my *personal* mount. And I'll tell you something, Mr. Long. I never loan him out to just anyone.''

"Well," Longarm replied, "if it makes you feel any better, I've never loaned Irma out to anyone either.''

Irma threw back her head and laughed. "Well, that's sure the gospel truth! And I wouldn't even let you do it now if Joe here wasn't so handsome.''

The compliment might have caused some men pleasure, but Joe just blushed all the deeper. Longarm took mercy on him by saying, "All right, let me see your horse.''

"He's in the barn," Joe said. "Follow me.''

Joe's horse was a paint, not Longarm's favorite choice of colors, but it really was a fine animal. He was a little jug-headed, but deep in the chest, with long, straight legs and a fine conformation.

"He goes like a locomotive," Joe said proudly. "He'll just keep huffing and puffing. Never slows down or gives up. You can hunt man or beast off of him, and he ground-ties. He'll pack meat and he's as sure-footed as a mountain goat. He can go days without rest or damn little feed and he doesn't bite, nor kick, nor buck.''

"I'll take him," Longarm said. "What's his name?"

"Splash."

"Fair enough," Longarm said. "Saddle Splash and

I'll tie what supplies I can behind the cantle and then be on my way."

"You won't get him shot, will you?"

"Not if I can help it."

"I paid eighty dollars for this horse and broke him of his bad ways. I've won money racing him in these mountains—he's that fast."

"I'll take good care of him. How is he around farm animals and cats?"

"He doesn't pay any attention to 'em," Joe quickly replied. "Oh, he'll stomp a dog if it gets under his feet. But that's about it."

"Saddle him," Longarm ordered. "I'm going to get us some breakfast and we'll be back in half an hour."

Joe licked his lips and swallowed hard. "Don't get lost, Miss Irma."

"Don't worry," she said, smiling sweetly, "I won't."

Longarm escorted Irma to breakfast. He was keeping an eye out for Elliot, worried that the fool might try to ambush him. But Elliot was nowhere to be seen, and Longarm figured he wouldn't be walking upright today anyhow since he'd been kicked so hard in the balls.

"You watch out for Elliot," he said to Irma. "He's crazy and you never know what a man like that will do to get even."

"He's not mad at me."

"Well, he's not very happy with you either," Long-arm replied as he found an empty table.

They had a good breakfast and Irma ate like a man. Longarm watched her closely and said, "You haven't been eating very well, have you?"

"I've been trying to earn and save enough money to quit the business, Custis."

"Go back to Denver and hole up at my place," he

said, dragging out a roll of greenbacks and handing them to her. "This ought to hold you for at least a month— if you don't spend it on clothes or whiskey."

She opened her mouth to say something, then closed it and looked down at her plate. "I suppose I have been drinking too much along with working too hard."

"It shows."

She looked up suddenly, her expression clouded with worry. "Does it really?"

"Yeah," Longarm replied, not wishing to be unkind but very much wanting her to know that he could see the physical toll her life was taking despite her youth and beauty. "Irma, find a job in Denver. An honest job."

"Like what?"

"Like working in a store. With your looks and personality, you could sell anything."

"You think so?"

"Sure!"

Irma slipped the money into her dress. "All right. I'll get a regular job and I'll even hold it until you return. I'll lay off the whiskey and get a lot of rest. And I'll eat right. You'll see me as a new woman and I'll be so dazzling to your sex-starved eyes that you'll probably propose marriage to me the minute we first meet."

He chuckled and set about finishing up his breakfast, saying, "That doesn't sound all bad. I'd like you to dazzle me, Irma. Even more than you already have."

Longarm was surprised to see tears spring to her eyes. "What's the matter?" he asked with concern.

"I dunno," she said, using a napkin to blow her nose. "I'm just not sure that I can ever change. I've been a whore so long that . . ."

"Shhhh!" Longarm whispered, reaching across the

table. "You're still a young woman. You're bright, fun, and beautiful. You turn men's heads and make us smile. Don't put yourself down anymore."

She sniffled. "Thanks, but I'm still a whore and I'll be doing it with Joe in a few more minutes."

Longarm stood up and paid his check. "To hell with that," he said gruffly. "I'll pay Joe for the use of Splash and you'll owe him nothing. How does that sound?"

Irma stood up and, oblivious of everyone in the place, threw her arms around his neck and kissed him, then hugged him tight. "I love you!" she shouted loud enough to be heard up and down the street.

Longarm loved her too. He wasn't going to get married, but Irma really mattered to him, and so he looked around the cafe proudly and then held out his arm. Together, they walked outside just as dignified as if he were the mayor of Jasper Rock and Irma was his proud wife.

Ten minutes later, he had paid Joe for the use of his paint and was on his way to Leadville. Joe looked devastated, but Irma was radiant. Maybe she would jump into the hay with Joe, but Longarm had a feeling that, if she did, she'd do it for free. Irma loved to make love and, well, moral judgments aside . . . that was just Irma being Irma.

Chapter 10

It was a fine morning and, if Longarm hadn't been in a big hurry to reach Leadville, he would have taken his time and enjoyed the ride. Splash was a spirited but sensible animal blessed with an easy jog, a soft lope, and a very fast walk, which was always appreciated. Longarm found that he liked Splash much better than Target, although he sort of missed the mule.

The mining road that he followed was empty except for an occasional ore wagon. Longarm passed several of these wagons as he began a steep climb up through heavily wooded country. To his right the mountain dropped off very sharply, and Longarm could see a glistening stream down in the gorge below. Once, he saw the wreckage of a big freight wagon and the bones of what had been its team of horses or mules. That didn't surprise Longarm because the drop-off was so steep.

He was about eight miles from Leadville and still admiring the views when an ambusher suddenly opened fire. Longarm felt the slug burn across his ribs, and then a second bullet creased his shoulder. Exposed without any nearby cover, he tried to leap from Splash, but the horse spun and sent him tumbling over the mountainside. Longarm attempted to stop his fall, but he was engulfed in a rolling, dust-boiling rock slide that carried him all the way to the bottom of the gorge and even a little way into the rushing stream. Battered, dazed, and bleeding, he lay still and half buried for several moments, trying to collect his wits and decide if he was severely injured or just banged up and bullet-creased in a couple of places.

He could still move his fingers and toes, which was a good sign, but the bad news was that everything except his head was covered with about two feet of rock.

"Damn!" he swore in the thick, choking dust as he struggled to dig himself out from under the blanket of shale that was still sliding across his body.

He finally managed to extract himself before the rock slide really cut loose and buried him alive. The dust was so thick Longarm couldn't see a thing, but he had no doubt that the ambusher was still up on the road and probably had his finger on the trigger of his rifle waiting for the dust to clear. With that in mind, it seemed imperative to Longarm that he find some cover and get hunkered down for whatever was to happen next.

But dammit, his six-gun was missing! He'd obviously lost it during his long, painful tumble down into this big gorge. Still coughing and choking in the heavy dust cloud, Longarm tied his bandanna around his face and began to crawl down to the stream, where he could hide among the shrubs and trees until he figured out who was out to fry his bacon.

A wild bullet probed the dust, but Longarm didn't

think he was in any danger as he crawled to the water and slipped in behind a big, mossy rock. He strained to look back up the slope, fearing that the ambusher might be coming right down after him. And while he had his derringer, it would be no match for either a rifle or a six-gun.

Sure enough, he saw a man coming down. Not directly, for the rock slide was slipping and only a complete fool would have attempted to descend from directly above. But about a hundred yards up the road, the slope was more manageable, and to Longarm's surprise, Elliot was coming down with a rifle clenched in his hands.

Longarm ducked and examined his wounds. He was all scraped up and his right knee was twisted so that he was not sure if he could even stand, much less run and hide somewhere upstream. His hands and face were cut and bleeding and the bullet wounds burned like a sonofabitch, but he was lucky to be alive and he wasn't complaining. Both slugs had just creased him, and Longarm supposed he ought to consider himself one lucky man. Or he would if this thing was settled. Unfortunately, Elliot was a determined cuss, in addition to having a pair of brass balls.

Longarm knew that he was in a poor hiding place and that Elliot would be able to spot and kill him, so there was little choice but to start moving downstream. With luck, maybe he could find a very good hiding place. One that Elliot would have to pass close enough to to give Longarm a good shot even with his inaccurate derringer.

Crabbing along the edge of the stream like a crawfish, Longarm felt panic rising in his chest. He kept glancing over his shoulder to see Elliot hurrying down the mountainside. The man was as agile as a mountain goat, and Longarm cussed himself for not giving Elliot a second boot in the balls. Anyone that ornery and determined had to be running on a pretty potent mixture of hatred.

Longarm couldn't stand and run. His twisted knee wasn't up to the strain, so the best that he could do was sort of scoot along the water, crawling over rocks and through heavy shrubbery. He was in a sea of pain and growing more desperate by the minute because damned if Elliot wasn't almost down the mountainside.

I have to find a place to hide and it had better be quick, he told himself, chest heaving with exertion.

And then sure enough, he heard the familiar slap of a beaver's tail striking water and knew that he was about to reach a pond. Longarm bulled his way through the thick brush and sized up the pond, which was long and quite deep. Longarm's first thought was to dive into the water. The pond was at least ten feet deep, and maybe he could bury himself in the mud and debris on the far side and thus avoid being detected.

"To hell with that," he decided out loud, knowing that it would eliminate any chance he had of using his derringer and putting a well-deserved end to Elliot's life.

Instead, Longarm chose to hobble along the edge of the pond and then duck behind the beaver's dam. There, he could have at least a half-decent chance of catching Elliot by surprise and at a close enough range to make use of his derringer.

The water was freezing as he waded into the stream below the dam and then leaned in close to the barricade of sticks and mud. He dared not raise his head because he didn't know how close Elliot was behind him. So he tried to block out the sound of the rushing water and listen hard for his pursuer.

Elliot wasn't very cautious. Longarm heard him coming from some distance. He was panting heavily and cussing under his breath. Twigs and limbs were snapping under his feet, and it was obvious that Elliot believed that he was chasing a dying man and had cast all caution aside.

Longarm's derringer was affixed to his gold watch chain, and it had saved his life on more than one desperate occasion. Trouble was, the two-shot derringer had no range at all. Beyond thirty feet . . . well, it all depended on luck.

Just sit tight and let him come to you, Longarm told himself. *Not that you have much choice.*

Elliot must have stopped at the top end of the beaver pond and realized that Longarm could have taken to the deeper water. Longarm eased his head up just a fraction of an inch above the uneven crest of the beaver dam and watched the revenge-crazed man study the still water.

"I'll find you, gawdammit!" Elliot screamed. His threat echoed around in the deep gorge. "You ain't getting away alive, you big bastard!"

That's what you think, Longarm grimly thought. *Come on and let's get this over with! I'm freezing down here and I haven't a clue as to how I'll get out once I put an end to your miserable life.*

"You might as well show yourself and get this over with!" Elliot bellowed. "I'll put a quick bullet in your head. I know you're hit and dying anyway. Be smart!"

Come on, come on!

Elliot turned very cautious as he began to skirt the beaver pond. Rifle held up and ready, he advanced very slowly. Longarm began to wonder if he'd chosen a very good ambush position after all. He'd just assumed that Elliot would come charging past the dam and become an easy target, but now it appeared that this was not going to happen. Because of his sudden caution, the odds had dramatically turned in Elliot's favor. Longarm was quite sure that, instead of running past him, Elliot was going to anticipate his hiding place and stay too far back to come within the range of the derringer. Longarm knew that he had to do something, and do it fast.

He bent over and selected a water-worn rock. Then, he found another and stuffed it into his pocket as his mind raced, still uncertain as to his next move.

A diversion. Make him turn and look away, then, somehow, try to rush him from behind and give yourself enough time to get within the derringer's range.

Longarm inched his head up just over the dam. Elliot was a real hunter, head swinging back and forth, every nerve in his body attuned to seeking his quarry. He was very close now. Another ten, maybe fifteen steps and he would reach the beaver dam. Longarm waited until Elliot's head swiveled away, and then he gritted his teeth and tossed a rock in a high, looping arc. It crashed into the brush causing Elliot to spin around and fire in a blind panic.

Longarm knew that he wasn't going to have a second chance to fool Elliot with a simple diversion, so he jumped forward, forcing himself to ignore the pain in his bum knee. His right hand gripped his derringer and he snatched the second rock out of his pocket as he charged full-tilt forward.

Elliot must have sensed his danger because he tried to pivot around and line his rifle up on Longarm. He'd have done it too if Longarm hadn't hurled his second rock, which struck Elliot in the chest and knocked him a half-step backward. Elliot shouted and tried to regain his balance and take aim, but he was a fraction too late and Longarm shot him at almost point-blank range. El-

liot gasped and staggered as Longarm shot him a second
time.

The man toppled over backward, his head striking a
rock and then slipping into the pond. Longarm retrieved
Elliot's rifle and pistol, then sat down to gather his wits
and catch his breath. He was all battered and messed up.
The bath that he'd never quite gotten around to taking
in Jasper Rock would have been a waste of time and
money.

Longarm tilted his head back to gaze up the steep
slope toward the road high above. He wasn't a bit sure
that he was going to be able to hike out of this gorge,
not with his bad leg. Well, he thought, there didn't seem
to be any choice but to try. Somewhere up there, Splash
might still be waiting along with Elliot's horse, which
would be hidden off the trail. So if Longarm could get
out, at least he'd have *two* horses, saddles, and rifles for
his trouble.

It took Longarm nearly three hours to crawl back out
of the gorge, and he had been fortunate to make it at
all. Luckily, he'd chanced upon a game trail, one with
solid footing. After that, it had just been a lot of grunting
and groaning until he'd finally made it back to the top.

Splash was gone, and so was Longarm's complete
outfit. Fortunately, it didn't take much time to discover
where Elliot had hidden his own animal, so Longarm
was able to mount up and ride back to the place where
he'd been ambushed. It appeared that several wagons
had passed on the road while he'd fought for his life
down in the gorge and then had struggled to climb out.
Reading the hoofprints as best he could, Longarm
thought it looked as if at least two of the passing wagons
had been heading for Leadville. One, however, had been
going back down to Jasper Rock.

Guess I'll go with the odds and hope that I can find my horse and outfit up ahead in Leadville, Longarm decided. If I can't, I suppose that I ought to feel grateful for Elliot's outfit, which isn't all that bad.

Longarm struggled into the saddle and rode on into Leadville, aware that every passerby was giving him a real going-over. That wasn't too surprising given that he was covered with dust and blood.

When he reached Leadville, he found the nearest livery and made hurried arrangements to have Elliot's horse boarded for the night.

"Mister," the liveryman drawled, "you look like you fell off a cliff or something."

"Well," Longarm said heavily, "that's just about what happened, all right. Have you seen a good-looking paint horse wearing a saddle and bedroll come into town?"

"An empty saddle?"

"That would be my guess."

"Well, then, as a matter of fact I have," the liveryman said. "He was tied behind an ore wagon. Reason I noticed was that he was one good-looking sonofabitch. I said to myself, 'Self, that there is a nice damn horse.' "

The man grinned. "That's what I said to myself, all right."

"Well," Longarm replied, "do you have any idea where I might be able to recover that paint?"

"He's yours?"

"He is."

"I'd look for him up at the Jim Bob Mining Company. That's where the ore wagon was heading."

"Where would that be?"

"About a mile up ahead."

"Thanks," Longarm said, climbing painfully back into the saddle.

"Mister, you don't look fit to ride up the street!" the liveryman called as Longarm started to ride away.

"I'm a fooler," Longarm called out as he put Elliot's horse into an easy jog on through town.

The Jim Bob Mining Company was just about what Longarm had expected, and he saw Splash still tied to one of the company's ore wagons up by the mining superintendent's office. Longarm rode up beside the paint and didn't even bother to dismount. Instead, he unbuckled his saddlebags and inspected them to make sure that nothing was missing. Everything was in place in both bags, but his rifle boot was empty, so Longarm figured he had no choice but to dismount and go inside the office in order to reclaim the rifle and get things straightened out.

"Hey!" a rough-looking man with a yellow bandanna tied around his thick neck called as he stormed outside. "Get away from that horse!"

"He's *my* horse," Longarm growled.

"The hell you say!"

"Where's my rifle?"

"What rifle?"

Longarm was in pain and completely out of sorts. He drew Elliot's six-gun and pointed it at the man's broad chest, saying, "As you can plainly see, I haven't had a very good day. So cut the bullshit and get my rifle before I put you under arrest . . . or worse."

The big man stared. "You're the *law*?"

"That's right," Longarm said angrily, reaching into a pocket filled with dust and pebbles to extract his badge. "A United States deputy marshal, and I could arrest you and probably have you *hanged* for horse stealing!''

The man actually threw up his hands as if he were under arrest. "Now hold on here, Marshal! I didn't steal that horse! I found him up wandering on the road and brought him in so him and your outfit would be safe.''

"The hell you say," Longarm snorted. "You meant to *keep* him! And I'll just bet anything you were in that office bragging to the boys that it was surely your lucky day.''

"No, I wasn't! Honest!''

Longarm had no wish to arrest the man, but he did want to put a good scare into him so that he'd handle things differently the next time. "Then why didn't you stop at the marshal's office in town and report the missing animal and outfit?''

"Well . . . well, I was just gonna do that! But first, I had a responsibility to my company to return my wagon and . . .''

"Aw, shut up," Longarm ordered. "Just get my damned rifle and shove it back in the boot and then get out of my sight.''

"You're not going to arrest me?''

"Depends on how quick you are," Longarm said.

The man darted inside the office and returned in a wink. He jammed Longarm's rifle into its scabbard and retreated, saying, "You better get yourself to a doctor! You don't look too damn good, Marshal!''

"I'm not too damn good," Longarm said, taking Splash's reins and leading the paint back into town.

Two hours later, he was soaking his poor bullet-creased, rock-bruised body in a hot bath, smoking a nickel cheroot, and sipping on some pretty good whiskey. The twisted knee had swollen up like a green gourd, and Longarm knew it would give him fits in the days just ahead. But he would mend. He always mended.

He also knew that there was a reasonably good-looking woman downstairs hoping he'd signal her to come up to his room for a vigorous romp in the sack, but Longarm wasn't at all up to that.

You're lucky, he thought, leaning his head back against the side of the tub and then closing his eyes, *just real damn lucky to be alive.*

Chapter 11

The Assassin had followed the Arkansas River and then the San Luis Creek, always heading south. He'd climbed over some damned high passes, and now he stopped and gave his horse a badly needed breather as he gazed down on South Park.

It was by any measure a huge valley, ringed on the east by the craggy Sangre de Cristo Mountains and on the west by the towering Continental Divide. As far as Jim Smith could see, South Park was carpeted with deep, lush grass and dotted with prosperous cattle ranches. Smith knew the winters up in this country were extremely severe, but spring, summer, and fall were so breathtaking that it probably made the winter struggle worthwhile. Even now, the cottonwoods following the valley's winding streams were starting to turn red and gold.

It doesn't get much prettier than this, Smith decided as he cocked his right knee around his saddlehorn and squinted against the bright afternoon sunshine. *Too bad that I have to come here for a killing.*

The Assassin wondered just how he was going to go about finding Red Skoal and the Ute woman. Smith didn't really want to just start riding from ranch to ranch because he knew that, in an isolated valley such as this, news traveled very fast. He would be willing to bet that Red Skoal would be warned long before he could be found. And without the element of surprise, Smith realized that his chances of successfully killing Skoal would be slim or none.

So, what to do next? There was a settlement in South Park. He could see it off in the distance, and knew that it was nothing but a general store, livery, hotel, cafe, two cowboy saloons, and one abandoned stage stop. The settlement would be the place to go. Once he was there, The Assassin was sure that a way to find Red Skoal would just naturally present itself. He'd always been lucky that way, just letting things come to him. And so, there again, it was a matter of patience. Patience, Smith knew, required courage and self-confidence. Without courage, men grew nervous and they invariably jumped into things that they ought to leave alone. They needed confidence that, given a little time, everything would come as it should.

Yep, patience was the main thing, but its underpinning was courage and confidence.

Three hours later and just about sundown, Smith rode into the little settlement and tied his horse in front of the busiest of the two ramshackle saloons. He started to go inside, then changed his mind and headed over to the cafe. There was a handful of men inside, but none of them was Red Skoal.

"Evening, stranger," the man wearing the apron

106

called. "You look like you could use a meal."

"I could," Smith agreed, smiling and trying to ignore the way that the damned cowboys were staring at his facial disfigurements. He pulled up his bandanna a little higher around his neck and marched over to a rickety little table with two chairs. Sitting down heavily with his back to the wall, he kicked his boots up on the second chair, cocked back his hat, and glared at the cowboys. When they kept looking at him, he growled, "What the hell are you boys staring at, gawdammit!"

There were four of them, all just kids really. That was why he excused them for their bad manners. But had any of them been foolish enough to give him a rude reply, he'd have had to administer a hard and painful lesson.

The cowboys suddenly got very interested in the subject of cattle, and Smith relaxed and called, "Mister, I'll have a *water* glass of whiskey."

"Coming right up!"

The whiskey was awful but it was in a big glass, and after the first shuddering swallow, it wasn't so awful anymore. The proprietor, a dumpy, balding man with a red, sun-ravaged face, said, "All I serve for supper is steak or venison or trout, along with potatoes and good bread."

"Steak and trout," Smith grunted. "Heavy on both and heavy on the bread and potatoes."

"Don't like venison, huh?"

"Not especially."

"I'll throw the steak on the fire, and the trout and potatoes are cooked and ready."

"Then bring 'em on," Smith said.

"Be a dollar and six bits first," the balding man said, looking nervous.

"That's a lot of damn money, and it better include another glass of whiskey."

"All right, sir."

Smith knew that he was being insulted by being asked to pay before his meal, but the whiskey was taking the edge off his anger and so he let the insult pass.

"Here you go," he said, digging the money out of his pocket and smacking it down on the table. "I like my steak a little bloody in the middle."

The man scooped up the money looking very grateful and relieved. The cowboys cleared out as soon as they could without looking like they were being intimidated, which they were. Smith knew that he must have made a pretty rough-looking figure of manhood what with his face and his guns and his dirty clothes. The thing of it was, he wanted to be ornery and crabby so that people wouldn't start asking him questions.

The trout was delicious and so was the rest of the meal, which seemed to arrive in shifts for about the next half hour. No one else entered the cafe, so it was just Smith and the proprietor, who when he wasn't bustling food over to Smith's table busied himself in the kitchen.

The Assassin took his time eating. He was in no hurry and the steak was tasty. When he finished, he enjoyed his second glass of whiskey almost as much as he had the first. The proprietor, it seemed, was a mite anxious to shut the cafe down. He looked like the kind of man who probably had a fat wife and three or four kids. Probably had even been a good cowboy in his younger days.

"How are cattle prices in this country?" The Assassin asked, wanting to start up a little conversation.

"Poor as usual. Ranchers hardly making any money."

"It's a tough business."

"It is," the proprietor agreed. "But then *life* is tough, even for the prayerful."

"Yeah," Smith said. "You owned this cafe long?"

"Nope."

"Like the business?"

"It's a living, barely. I got regulars. I was a cook on the Rocking B Ranch. You know where that is?"

"In this valley?"

"No, down near Taos, New Mexico."

"Huh," Smith grunted. "I should have known that because me and Red used to work down that way."

"Red Skoal?"

"Yeah. I lost track of him, but heard he'd settled in these parts."

The proprietor brightened a little. "Hell, yes, he did! Red comes in here a couple times a week to take his supper. He likes his steak just the same as you and he's not afraid of that whiskey either."

Smith chuckled. "Yeah, he always was quite a fella. I haven't seen him in . . . oh, six or seven years."

"Well, then, you ought to stop by his place."

"I'm on my way to Santa Fe."

"Red likes company. He's got a pretty nice little spread out at the south end of this valley. If you're aimin' for Santa Fe, you'll be riding that way anyhow."

"Yeah, I guess that I would be," Smith said as if the idea would never have occurred to him. "Trouble is . . ."

"What?"

"I'm sort of down and out right now. Haven't got much money, and my clothes . . ."

"Aw," the man scoffed, "you know Red! He's pretty rough-looking himself and he don't give a damn about how anybody looks. Why, I heard it told that he once—''

''You think he'd put me up for the night?'' Smith interrupted. ''I hate to spend the last of my money on a hotel room.''

''Sure he would! Probably give you a job too! He's already got two or three hands, but they're mostly all butt-broke cowboys that would rather drink and play cards in his bunkhouse than do any real work.''

''How many cattle does Red own?''

''Oh, maybe five hundred. He's not a big-time rancher, but he does all right. Always seems to have money, even when cattle prices have gone to hell like they have right now.''

''He must have a rich uncle or something.''

The proprietor came over and drew up a chair. ''Don't tell Red that I said so, but he has some 'side businesses' that aren't exactly legal.''

''Like rustlin'?''

''Oh, hell, no! Every cowboy in South Park knows every cow in South Park as well as he knows his own sister. No, you couldn't steal a one without everyone knowin' it. But Red, he likes to ride out and nobody rightly knows what he does, but he comes back with money. Not that I'm saying he's a thief or anything! Hell, no.''

''Not Red,'' Smith agreed. ''He's honest as the day is long.''

''Well,'' the man said, ''I don't know about that. Red tells me that he goes off and gambles down in Taos or even over in Denver. And he *is* one hell of a good poker player. He can deal a deck of cards, I tell you. Why, he's so good they don't even let him play in the games at the saloons.''

"Is that a fact?"

"Sure is! Red almost always wins."

"No man's luck runs that pure," Smith said. "He must give it a little nudge with a card off the bottom or someone other such thing."

"I expect so, but Red isn't a man to be accusin' of anything. If he's drinkin' or feelin' low, he'll shoot a man without needing much of a reason."

"And there's no law up here to arrest him."

"That's right! So people just sort of tread easy around Red. If you know what I mean."

"Sure I do." Smith sipped his whiskey. "Red ever get married?"

"Nope, but he's got a real handsome Indian. Her name is Betty and she's a half-blooded Ute. Damn pretty woman too. Red once killed a man that stared at Betty too long. Did it right across the street in front of the hotel. Now nobody so much as sneaks a peek at Betty."

"Thanks for the warning," Smith said.

"Oh, if you're old friends, I guess Red will cut you some extra slack. Just don't stare at Betty, and when Red starts to drinking real bad, find somewhere else to be. Understand?"

"I sure do," Smith said, dropping his feet from the empty chair and standing. He patted his distended belly, saying, "That was a real fine meal."

"Glad you liked it. Stop by again the next time that you are passing though and say hello."

"I will," Smith promised.

"And don't let them cowboys get you on the prod. They're just dumb kids. We don't see a lot of strangers up here, so they have a tendency to gawk a little."

"Sure," Smith said, belching and heading for the

111

door. "What did you say the name of his ranch was? The Rocking B?"

"Naw, that's the ranch that *I* worked on down in New Mexico. Red's ranch is called the Bar S. It's the last one on the south end of this valley. He's got some big cotton-woods planted around a nice house and has a big barn with a bunch of busted-down wagons all around. His dog is a hound and he'll wail when he sees you comin' into the yard."

"I'll find it."

"You can't miss it. Just stay to the road and it's the last spread on the right. And say hi to Red and Betty for me . . . well, Red anyway."

"I'll do it," The Assassin said as he went out and climbed onto his waiting horse. "You just damn sure bet on that."

Chapter 12

The moon was up and the coyotes howling by the time The Assassin reached the end of South Park. He reined his horse in beside a tiny weathered sign, and had to strike a match to read a Bar S brand burned in wood.

Smith shook his head. "Not too impressive for a ranch sign. I'm thinkin' that you don't want to attract any passin' strangers, huh, Red?"

The cottonwoods were bathed in moonlight, and Smith could see lamplight in the windows of the Bar S ranch house, which was located about a half mile from the road. The dark silhouettes of busted wagons reminded Smith of animal carcasses he'd seen one spring after a real bad Montana winter.

They got a hound dog, Smith thought. *That fella at the cafe said they had a hound dog and he'll start bayin' just as soon as I put a foot on their property. I can bet on that. So what should I do? Hole up and wait for Skoal to come to town and then ambush him? Be less risky than riding up there in the dark and givin' him some warning.*

Smith yawned. He shouldn't have had those two water glasses of whiskey because they'd made him sleepy. He wasn't in any shape for a gunfight, that was for certain.

Smith drummed his heels against his horse's ribs and continued on down the road to the end of South Park. Then he reined west and made his horse pick its way through the rocks and the pines. He would hole up somewhere in these mountains, up and behind Skoal's ranch house. He had food and water. He could wait out Red for a day or even two. By then, he was sure that Skoal would unwittingly offer himself as a target. After that, he'd go down to the ranch and maybe even have some fun with Betty.

Smith slept late on his soft bed of pine needles. The sun was high on the eastern horizon when he pushed himself up to his elbows and scrubbed the sleep from his eyes. He stretched, yawned, and climbed stiffly to his feet, eager to get a good look at the Bar S Ranch spread.

The house was bigger than he'd judged last night, and it had a nice front porch. Most interesting, however, was the activity that was taking place in the ranch yard. Smith moved a little further down the hill and then sat on a rock. He squinted into the morning sun and saw that there were three men at work on one of the old wagons, which was missing a wheel. A fourth man—or maybe the Ute woman—was over by the corral saddling a black horse.

It was almost impossible to tell which of the men below was Red Skoal. The outlaw was of average size and build so he didn't stand out any. He had reddish brown hair and a beard, but everyone in sight was wearing a hat and three of them had beards.

The Assassin hunkered down to await what would transpire. By and by, the one with the black horse rode off with a dog following along behind. They were heading north. The dog was big with short hair, and Smith figured it was the hound. An hour passed before Smith moved back up to his camp to feed his horse a bait of oats. He ate some dried beef and hardtack, and wished he could light a fire and boil some coffee. Fortunately, the day was warm, but there were some dark storm clouds to the north. Unless he was reading the signs wrong, Smith figured it was going to storm. Well, that was fine too. By then, he'd be in Red Skoal's house, most likely also in his bed enjoying the Ute Indian woman.

About mid-morning, the three bearded men in the ranch yard got a wheel on the busted wagon and two of them hitched it up. Smith watched as they loaded the wagon with coils of barbed wire and a dozen or so cedar fence posts. The three stood around and talked for about ten minutes, one of them pointing and gesturing. Then the other two climbed into the wagon and drove off.

I'm in luck, Smith thought as he watched the man he judged to be Skoal disappear into the sagging barn. *The woman and the hound are gone and so is the hired help. Now it's just Red and me.*

The Assassin saddled and bridled his horse. He checked his weapons and took a couple of deep breaths. Besides the rifle in his saddle scabbard and the Colt on his hip, he had another revolver, which he shoved into his coat pocket. That would be the surprise if he needed to get the drop on Red Skoal.

There being no time to waste, Smith broke camp and

mounted his horse. He reined it down the steep mountainside, keeping to the trees for as long as possible and never taking his eyes off the barn, house, or ranch yard. With any luck, he might make it all the way to the barn before Skoal even realized he had a very unwelcome visitor. It didn't hurt that there was also a little gully that would keep him out of view until he was almost into the ranch yard.

Smith could feel a rising sense of anticipation building up like steam in a locomotive's boiler. He pushed his horse into a trot, and when he came to the end of the gully, he dismounted and hurried ahead on foot, dropping his reins and sprinting directly for the barn. Chest heaving, he stopped just outside the door. Smith heard a man inside whistling an unfamiliar tune. Red sounded happy, and that filled Smith with a killing rage because his own wife and son had also been happy until they'd been murdered.

Smith drew his holstered six-gun, deciding to just step inside and open fire. Unfortunately, however, the light was very bad inside and he knew that his eyes would need several minutes to adjust, while Skoal's eyes would give him the advantage. It was enough to give Smith second thoughts. He closed his eyes and weighed his next move.

Patience, he told himself. *Just wait and Skoal will come outside. He has to, sooner or later. And when he does, you will have the advantage and it'll be his eyes that will need to make the adjustment.*

Smith forced himself to relax. He leaned against the barn, listening to Skoal whistle and bang away with his hammer. It sounded as if the outlaw-rancher might be repairing a stall. Smith didn't know nor did he really

116

care. The main thing was that he had patience and was biding his time.

Ten minutes passed, then twenty. Smith was growing impatient. *What if the two men on the wagon suddenly appeared? They would see his saddled horse wandering around in the yard and become alert. Or what if the woman on the horse and her damn dog suddenly appeared? That would also destroy his element of surprise.*

You have to do something now, he thought. *You don't have the luxury of waiting any longer for Skoal to stop whistling and banging around inside before he steps through this damn barn doorway.*

The Assassin squared his shoulders and slipped around the corner of the barn door, gun waving in front of him like a dark finger of death. Skoal's back was turned and he was oblivious to any danger.

"Hello, Red."

Skoal pivoted, hammer in hand. Only it wasn't Skoal! It was a stranger, and now he took a few steps forward, saying, "Red is out fixin' fence right now. He'll be back come sundown and . . . what's that in your hand, mister?"

"A gun."

The ranch hand drew in his breath sharply, then retreated, dropping his hammer and throwing his hands high up in the air. "Do you mean to *rob* me? I ain't got no money!"

Smith had always prided himself as a quick-thinking man. He didn't want to kill this ranch hand, but then again, he couldn't really allow him to live.

"Keep your hands up!"

"Sure! But mister, this is a real *poor* spread. Nobody here has any cash."

"Turn around slow."

117

"Please don't shoot me."

"Turn around!"

"All right! But I ain't never hurt nobody. Honest. And I got two dollars in my jeans. You can have all of it. Just *please* don't kill me!"

"Shut up!"

He was maybe twenty, a big, homely kid with buck teeth and straw-colored hair. He was scared so bad his upraised hands were shaking.

"Oh, hell," Smith swore, pistol-whipping the kid across the back of his head and sending him sprawling across the dirt floor. Smith bent down and felt for a pulse, knowing he might have killed the kid. There was a pulse, so Smith found some rope in the barn and hog-tied him. The kid would be out cold for most of the day and he was going to have one hell of a bad headache, but at least he'd be alive.

Smith dragged the ranch hand into the dim stall that he'd been repairing. He pitched some straw over the kid, then hurried outside to catch up his horse, which had wandered over to a corral where it was getting acquainted with some other ranch horses. He led the animal into Red's barn, where it could not be seen by anyone.

When Smith was satisfied that his horse would not be giving his presence away, he took his rifle and went to inspect the ranch house. It was surprisingly nice, with comfortable horsehide couches and a big rack of elk antlers mounted over the mantle. There were bear skins and cowhides on the floor and the house was very clean. A colorful Indian headdress was tacked to one wall, and a warrior's spear rested proudly on another. Those would be Betty's touch.

Suddenly, Smith heard the hound bark. He whirled

and raced to the front door just in time to see the Indian woman come loping into the yard with the dog in the lead. She hadn't a clue of any danger. The hound dropped its snout to the dirt and quickly caught Smith's foreign scent. A moment later, it sensed his location and charged the house.

Smith waited until the big hound was almost to the porch before he shot it in the face. It was a good shot, and the dog's snout plowed dirt and it somersaulted, dead before it came to a rest.

The Indian woman wasn't armed. She saw Smith and tried to rein around and escape, but Smith shot her horse. The woman fell hard under her thrashing mount, and then cried out in pain as the dying horse landed on her leg, pinning it to the earth.

Smith ran over and shot the dying horse. The woman tried to pull herself free, but couldn't. She *was* pretty, all right. Pretty as could be with shiny black hair, beautiful brown skin, and large dark eyes. Her free leg was long and slender. He could see that, even though she was wearing a man's pants and shirt.

"Just rest easy," Smith cautioned, leaning his rifle against the porch. "I'll grab the saddlehorn and when I lift, you pull away. Can you do that?"

Betty didn't say anything. She didn't have to. Her hate-filled eyes told Smith everything he needed to know. Smith had seen animals caught in the steel jaws of a trap that looked happier than this Ute woman, but he still could not leave her pinned under the horse. He bent over to grab her saddlehorn and lift enough weight of the dead animal to free the woman. But then he heard the drumming of racing hooves.

"I'm going to have to leave you here until I take care of your friends," he said.

She spat at him.

"That wasn't very ladylike," he said, picking up his rifle. "But then, you *aren't* a lady, are you?"

She spat again. Smith didn't have time to bother with her, so he levered another shell into his rifle and sprinted back to the barn. He skidded to a halt, put his rifle to his shoulder, and waited.

Red Skoal and his ranch hand were both in the wagon when it flew past Smith into the ranch yard. They damn near ran over Betty and her fallen horse. Skoal had to really haul up on the lines, causing the wagon to slew around on two wheels and catapulting him and his ranch hand into the air. The ranch hand struck the side of the house and was knocked unconscious. Red also struck the house, but was only dazed. He tried to stand while fumbling for his sixgun.

The Assassin shot the murdering sonofabitch in the belly. Red screamed and crashed over backward, arms beating at the earth like broken wings. Smith strolled over to the outlaw and levered another cartridge into his Winchester. He planted his legs wide apart and pointed the rifle at Red's bloodless face.

"Who *are* you?" the outlaw choked as a trickle of blood spilled from the corner of his mouth and ran into his beard.

"Funny you should ask, because your friend Hank Trabert asked me the very same question before I finished him off like I'm going to finish you off."

"I don't . . . understand! Whoever you are, at least give me a fighting chance!"

"Sure," Smith drawled, smiling murderously. "I'll give you exactly the same chance that you gave my family when you burned them up in Denver."

Smith leaned forward, then jammed the barrel of his

rifle into Red's mouth so hard he split the man's lips and broke through his front teeth. "Burn in hell, Red!"

He squeezed the trigger and blew the back of Red's head off. It wasn't pretty, but it was far more merciful than the man deserved. "I would have burned *you* alive if it hadn't been for the Ute woman needing attention," Smith told the body.

The woman was still struggling to tear herself free. Her pretty face reflected intense pain.

Smith squatted on his heels out of spitting range. "Betty," he began, "I want to tell you something before I try to lift this horse off that leg. I killed Red because he was part of the bunch that murdered my wife and son. He was no damn good."

Betty stopped struggling, eyes still radiating venom.

"And," Smith continued, "I'll tell you something else. If you try to turn on me after I free you up, I'll kill you too. I don't want to. I didn't kill the fella in the barn, nor will I kill the one that slammed into the house—if you behave and act decently. I'll expect good food and a courteous manner. After supper, we'll sleep together. Is that understood?"

She stopped squirming. "I understand."

"Then you'll act like a lady?"

"A . . . a lady?"

"That's right. I'll get you into the house, do my best to care for that leg, but you got to act like a lady."

Betty swallowed hard and finally nodded. "I think my leg is broken."

"Let's hope not," he told her as he laid his rifle down and grabbed the saddlehorn. "All right, we'll do this on the count of three. One. Two. Three!"

Smith managed to raise the carcass just enough so that Betty could pull free.

"Good," he said, reaching down and pulling her up. "Can you walk?"

She tried, but crumpled in pain.

"All right, then," he said, easing her back to the ground. "I'm going to tie this other fella up, if he's still alive. After that, I'll carry you into the house and cook for the both of us. I'm real hungry. Are you?"

She didn't answer, so he left her to wait. The man who'd been thrown from the wagon was dead with a broken neck, which made things simpler all the way around. Smith went back to the Ute woman, scooped her up, and headed into the ranch house. Placing her on one of the horsehair couches, he busied himself in the kitchen, cooking them a fine big meal. He also found Red Skoal's supply of whiskey. Smith was in good spirits as he kept one eye on his meal and the other on the pretty Ute woman.

"How'd you ever wind up keeping company with a snake like Red?" he finally asked.

"He once killed a bad man for me."

"Oh." Smith gazed into the fire. "I suppose that he also gave you a lot of presents and treated you well too."

"Yes."

"He was a murderer and a thief," Smith snapped. "You must know that he rode with the Marble brothers, who are just about as rotten as they come."

"My leg is hurting bad."

"Here, drink some of Red's whiskey. It's rough, but it'll ease the pain."

Betty drank it straight. Smith shook his head. "A lady always ought to drink from a glass, not the damn bottle."

"I told you, I'm no lady. Don't *want* to be no gawdamn lady either!"

"At least you're honest."

"What are you going to do about my leg?"

"What do you want me to do?"

"Splint it. Get me to a doctor."

"I'll splint it, but I'm not riding for a doctor. I got others to hunt for."

"Joe and Dave Marble?"

"That's right."

"Are you going to try and kill them too?"

"I am."

She managed a thin smile. "I'll be happy when they kill you instead."

"Not too much chance of that," he replied. "I'll shoot 'em just as dead as I did old Red Skoal and that sonofabitchin' Trabert. There's a fella named Jake Mill that is supposed to live over by Cortez. I mean to kill him too."

"He's mean."

"That gang was *all* mean."

"Red was always real good to me." Betty's eyes glistened with tears.

"Hard to figure a man out sometimes," Smith admitted. "But the fact that he was good to you don't matter none to me. I should have made him suffer instead of killing him so fast. I . . . I showed no patience."

"You're crazy."

"Maybe I am. But you better be nice to me or only one of us is going to make it through this night."

Betty met his eyes and then she looked away, whispering, "I'll be *real* nice to you, mister. But first, you got to splint my gawdammn leg so the bone don't set crooked.''

"Be a pleasure," he said, grinning wolfishly before heading back outside to find a flat, straight board and some binding.

Chapter 13

"You're leg isn't broken," Smith announced after a careful examination. "It's purple and swollen bad—probably hurts like hell—but I'm sure that it's not broken."

"How can you be so sure?"

"My father was a country doctor," Smith answered. "I used to make the rounds with him when I was young. I've seen a lot of blood and broken bones, but I'm not looking at either right now."

"Your father was a *doctor*?"

"That's right," Smith replied. "He even went to medical school. He wanted me to become a doctor and take over his practice after he finally retired. But I wanted nothing to do with that."

"So your father saved lives but you take them," the woman said.

"That's right. When I was fourteen my father was called out in the night to attend to a man who had been shot in the leg with a scattergun. It was a terrible wound and he had to amputate if he was to save the man's life.

"Trouble was, my father couldn't stop the bleeding as he began to cut the leg off. The man was a bleeder and he died screaming and cursing. His two brothers, who were off getting drunk in town, blamed my father."

Smith took a deep, ragged breath and his eyes grew hard and distant as he continued to speak. "About midnight, they both rode home to find my father and their dead brother. They went crazy, then shot and badly wounded my father. After that, they had some fun carving his legs off at the knees. I heard they laughed as he bled to death."

Betty shivered. "They sound like terrible men."

"They were," Smith choked. "My father did his level his best but they killed him anyway. So I killed them."

"You? A boy?"

"Yes," Smith said.

"But how?"

"Even back then, I had a fascination for guns and spent a lot of time and my father's money on target practice. My father didn't like it much, but he wasn't so naive that he didn't understand that a man sometimes had to be able to defend himself. So after he was shot and butchered, I went after those two brothers. The first one died quick with a look of amazement that I'll never forget. He just couldn't believe that he'd been shot down by a fourteen-year-old kid."

"And what of the second one?"

"I met him down at the train yard in Abilene, Kansas. He was a wrangler in the stock pens . . . when he was sober. I braced him in a stand-up fight and easily beat him to the draw. I shot him in both knees, and he screamed so loud that hundreds of wild Texas longhorn

126

cattle broke down their fences. He begged for his life but . . .''

''But you *had* to kill him, didn't you?''

''That's right,'' Smith said quietly. ''The more bullets I put into him and the more he screamed, the madder I got. Finally, I just shot him between the eyes. Much like I'd killed snakes or varmints. I took his money, guns, and horse, then rode away. Nobody tried to stop me. They were all much too scared.''

''And no one ever came after you?''

''No,'' Smith answered, ''because I left Kansas far behind and rode up to Montana and became a shotgun guard for a stage line. Later, I went to work for the marshal in Cheyenne. I was good, and eventually became the law there. But despite everything I could do, I kept killing men and liking it more and more. I guess you could say I developed a lust for blood.''

''You didn't kill Randy out in our barn! At least, you told me you didn't.''

''No, I didn't kill him,'' Smith agreed. ''He was too young and afraid. I had to let him live.''

''And you let *me* live.''

''Why, sure! I'm not a monster. I've killed plenty of men, but all of them were bad and deserved to die. I just saved the law the trouble of arresting them and then having a damned trial. I figure that I've saved the taxpayers a lot of money over the years by killing men that deserved to die.''

''Do you expect to go on killing? I mean, after you get the rest of the Marble Gang?''

''I hope not,'' he answered. ''I realize that my luck must some day run dry. And I expect that the federal government is after me. They've probably got men on

127

my trial right now. That's why I've got to finish off this business and then disappear.''

She frowned. ''How, exactly, do you do that?''

''You change your name.''

''That can't be enough.''

''No, there's more to it than that. I've put plenty of thought to the matter during the past few months. I expect that I'll pick out a small, quiet town and take a lowly job swamping out saloons or working in a livery. I'll join a church and work hard. I won't drink in saloons, and I'll ask to be a volunteer fireman or any other thing I can do to gain trust among the town leaders. After a year, maybe two, I'll have earned their complete respect.''

''You can't live on respect alone,'' she told him. ''And I don't think a man like you can be so poor and humble for very long.''

He allowed himself a smile. ''You're a pretty fair judge of a man, aren't you?''

''I don't know . . . anymore.''

''Well,'' he said, ''you're right about me. I like money and I'm not one to sit in the wings and let other men run my life. But I'll do it, by gawd, for a time. And all the while, I'll be saving up money. In a few years, two or three at the most, I'll have enough saved to buy my own business.''

''What kind of business?''

''The profitable kind.''

''And what then?''

He shrugged. ''I don't know. Maybe some day I'll run for the mayor of the damn town, but I doubt it. I've never had any interest in politics. You have to speak with a forked tongue and shake hands with your enemies.''

"Men you would rather shoot."

"Yeah, but I won't," he vowed. "Not anymore. I'll turn over a new leaf. I'll grab ahold of respectability and not pick up a gun except to defend myself, my family, or my friends."

"So, you will have another family?"

He reached out and touched her cheek. "Looking at you like this, I realize that I have to have a wife and . . . and maybe even try to have children again. I don't know. It's all too sudden to think about those kinds of things."

"I've never met anyone like you before. You're crazy and dangerous, but you are good too."

"I *am* a little crazy," he admitted. "You've got that part right. I can't figure out why I get so much satisfaction from killing evil people or punishing those who are rude or bullies. But I do and I can't deny the fact."

"Do you ever have nightmares about all the men you've killed?"

"No."

"How many *have* you killed?"

"I don't keep count."

"More than ten, though," she said. "You've killed way more than ten men."

"Yeah. Way more."

"When are you going after the brothers?"

"I'd like to stay here for a day or two and rest. But I better go tomorrow morning."

He stripped down to his long underwear and examined her leg one last time. "It'll be fine in a week. You just need to keep off of it as much as you can until the swelling goes down."

"All right."

"I'll sleep in the other bedroom tonight."

She watched him limp stiffly away. And then, for reasons Betty did not even try to understand, she left her bed and hopped into the other bedroom to be with him all through the night.

The Assassin slept late. He awoke to hear the Ute woman bumping around in the kitchen. She was humming and he could smell pork cooking.

Betty could have gotten up, found a butcher knife, and put an end to me, he thought. *She could have killed me in my sleep. Cut my throat or done anything she wanted. But she's cooking us breakfast and damned but isn't it nice to hear a woman humming in the kitchen again.*

Smith crawled out of bed and washed the sleep from his eyes. He was astounded that the Ute woman would be up and around. She had to be in considerable pain. But then again, he recalled that his father had once told him that some people had an enormous capacity for blocking out pain. They could just put it out of their minds and go about their business. Others, however, were always moaning and groaning over even the slightest discomfort.

Smith pulled on his clothes, thinking about how he and the woman had not made love but had lain close in each other's arms. It had been very good just like that, and he had slept better than he had since losing his family.

"Hey," he called, standing in the doorway. "You're not supposed to be up and about!"

"My leg feels a lot better this morning," she told him with a smile. "And I was hungry."

"So am I," he said, marching over to drop down at the kitchen table. "Maybe, if you cooked some extra, I could take it along for my next few meals."

"I've thought of that," she said. "I want to go with you."

"No."

"I'm coming," she said without equivocation. "I know those people. I can help you."

"I don't need any help."

"You do this time."

"You can hobble around in this kitchen, but you can't ride a horse."

"Did you see the buggy in the barn?" she asked, coming over to pour him a cup of coffee. "We could take that."

"Yesterday, you hated me. I saw it in your eyes. And you said that I was crazy."

"You are only a little crazy."

"Then you should stay here."

"And spend the rest of my life wondering what happened to you? I don't like that idea."

"You just can't come," he said. "This ranch, who does it belong to now?"

"To me."

"Good! Then stay here and settle in. Find an honest husband. One who doesn't kill a lot of men and who will make you happy."

"Last night, *you* made me happy," she said, limping over to sit down beside him. "I saw something in you that I like."

"You *saw* me kill Red. It was pretty ugly, Betty. That's a side of me that not many have seen and lived to tell about."

"Maybe we could come back here and live."

He laughed, but it was a cold, hard laugh without humor. "Have you forgotten that there are *two* dead men in your yard and another that is hog-tied in the barn?

131

What do you think he's going to do if I let him go?''

"I don't know. Randy is a good boy. He likes me."

"Not enough to hide my murder."

Smith reached out and took her hands. "It's just no good, Betty. I don't know why you were here and what happened to us last night. How you went from hate to . . . to something completely opposite. But I can't stay here at your Bar S Ranch. There will be federal officers after me and they may be here today."

When she said nothing, he added, "If you *really* want to help me, send them off on a wild-goose chase."

"You *need* me to be with you when you face those brothers!"

"After six months have passed, I'll write to you. You can come to see me."

"You won't *live* six months! Not if you go after those men by yourself."

Smith drank some coffee. "Let me think on this a little while. I'll bury Red and that other one out in the trees somewhere and cover their graves with leaves and pine needles. After that, we'll talk some more. Okay?"

She nodded. "You need to eat something."

"Yes," he said, "I do."

"And after you bury them, you check on Randy. He's not a bad boy."

"I know."

"And then we can go back to bed," she told him. "We will make love this time."

"In broad daylight?"

"Yes." Betty touched his cheek, then ran her fingers down to his scarred neck. "And after we do that, you will decide that we should go away together."

Smith didn't have the heart to refuse her. "All right," he said, "we'll do it your way and see what happens."

"Good!" She jumped up, and soon had a big plate of pancakes and pork chops before him. Then she filled a plate for herself, and together they ate enough for five hard-working men.

Chapter 14

By the time that Longarm tracked The Assassin to the Bar S Ranch in South Park, the man had already left two men in the town's little cemetery and the Ute woman named Betty had simply disappeared.

"He seemed like a nice enough fella," Tom Blanton, who owned the little cafe, said. "Of course, with those red burn scars down on his neck and all, he did stand out some."

"What about the rest of his face?" Longarm asked. "Had that also been disfigured?"

"Not at all. When he was here, he wore a bandanna wrapped up close under his chin, sort of like a cowboy will do in bad riding weather. He's a handsome kinda fella and sure had me fooled. I can't tell you how bad I feel about giving him directions so he could ride out and kill Red and one of his hired hands."

Longarm listened with great interest as Tom explained how The Assassin had pistol-whipped a kid named

Randy. Then he said, "I'd like to talk to Randy, if possible."

"Sure, he's staying at the hotel. He should go to Denver or Santa Fe and see a doctor."

"Why?"

"Well, he's not doing so good," the man said with a worried expression. "He really took a vicious blow to the head and he still seems a little dazed. Randy tells me that he's having some really fierce headaches."

"He probably had a concussion," Longarm said. "I've had a couple of them myself."

"You have?"

"That's right. The skull gets cracked and the brain bruised. The aftereffects, namely headaches, can plague a man for months, but he'll generally have a full recovery."

"You ought to tell Randy that. He's real down and afraid he'll never be able to work again."

"I'll go see him," Longarm promised. "Maybe he'll recall something important."

"Maybe," Tom said, "but I wouldn't count on it. He's in rough shape. Lost weight and seems . . . well, he used to be a pretty happy kid."

"What did he do for Red Skoal?"

"General ranch work."

Longarm found it difficult to believe that anyone working for Red would not have been involved in theft of some kind, but there wasn't any point in saying that to this man.

So after his meal, he went over to the hotel and looked up young Randy Thomas, who was sitting in the lobby attempting to read a week-old newspaper. After the introductions, Longarm sat down with the kid and studied him closely.

"They say that you took a bad blow to the head and are having headaches."

"I am," Randy admitted. "It's been more'n a week now and I still feel real bad. Don't know if I'll ever get back to my old self."

"I expect that you get dizzy too," Longarm said, "especially when you stand up too fast."

"I do!" Randy frowned. "How'd you know that?"

"I've had a few hard knocks to the head myself. And I wanted to tell you that you *will* fully recover. When you are hit that hard, the doctors tell me you either suffer permanent brain damage and usually die, or you fully recover. You're definitely going to recover."

The kid brightened. "I sure am glad to hear that. I was just thinking that I might be all washed up with no way to support myself."

"You'll be fine." Longarm leaned closer. "Tell me exactly what happened."

In halting words, the kid told Longarm about the few moments he'd seen The Assassin and then how he'd been ordered to turn around and how he didn't remember anything after that.

"The light wasn't good, so I'm not even sure that I'd recognize that sonofabitch if I ever saw him again."

"What do you think happened to the woman?"

"You mean Betty?"

"Yes."

"He probably pistol-whipped her too. Then he must have forced her to go with him. She wouldn't have ever gone by choice."

"Why do you say that?"

"Because," Randy said, "Betty loved the Bar S. And I heard Red once say that she stood to inherit the spread if anything happened to him."

"Do you know if he had a will made out?"

"No."

"Do you know the Marble brothers?"

"I . . . I guess I do."

"And there's a fella named Jake Mill that was a member of their gang. I'm told that he lives in Cortez."

"Could be he does."

Longarm's voice hardened. "Don't play games, Randy! The man who pistol-whipped you and took that woman has already killed Hank Trabert and his father and brother, and now he's killed Red and the hand with the broken neck."

"Johnny. His name was Johnny Webb."

"All right. So this man, The Assassin, has killed five men since I've started tracking him out of Denver, and there are three more members of the Marble gang that have no idea that their lives are in real danger. Maybe I can arrest The Assassin before he completes what he has set out to do. But I need to know anything you can tell me. Mostly, I need to know where this Jake Mill and the Marble brothers are so that I can get to them before The Assassin does."

"Is *that* what you call him? The Assassin?"

Longarm dipped his chin. "For lack of a better name."

"Well," Randy said, "I can't tell you a thing more than I already have."

Longarm gazed deep into the kid's troubled eyes and figured he was telling the truth. "Randy," he said, coming to his feet, "you're going to be all right. But maybe you should go to Denver and see a doctor, just in case."

"Got no money."

"Can you get someone to take you?"

"I suppose, but . . ."

Longarm scribbled Billy Vail's name and the address of the Federal Building where he and Billy worked. "You look up my boss and give him a letter that I'm about to write. Tell him that I'm heading for Cortez and that The Assassin has killed Red and Trabert and is after Jake Mill and the Marble brothers."

"I'll do that, but . . ."

"Here," Longarm said, digging a roll of bills out of his pocket and counting out some money, then scribbling down the name of a Dr. Marston with a busy medical practice in Denver. "There's thirty dollars and the name of a good doctor. You tell him I sent you. And as for Billy, well, he's got a reputation for being a very soft touch and he'll also help you out."

"Why are you doin' this for me?"

"Because I know how bad you feel," Longarm replied. "And because if I'd gotten to The Assassin, you wouldn't be in such pain."

"Weren't your fault."

"Maybe, maybe not," Longarm said. "But anyway, go to Denver and have your head checked out."

"I got a friend that lives there. Maybe he'll let me stay the winter and when I get better, I can get a job again. Ain't no work up here in South Park."

"Then good luck to you," Longarm said.

"You're the one that's going to need the luck!"

"I guess you're right."

"Maybe Betty will kill him for you. She's a tough one."

"Maybe. If he doesn't kill her first."

"You think she's already dead?"

Longarm gave the question some thought, then shook his head. "No, I don't," he answered. "This man is a killer, but he seems to have some regard for children and for women. Could be that you're alive today because you're so young.''

Randy cradled his head in his rough, calloused hands. ''Since it happened, I been wondering if I wouldn't have been better off dead.''

''Don't even talk like that,'' Longarm said. ''Get to the doctor. After he examines you, I'm sure that you'll feel a lot better about your future.''

Randy nodded. ''How long will these headaches go on?''

''Could be another few weeks.''

''I'm half tempted to stay drunk.''

''Now that,'' Longarm assured Randy, ''would only make the headaches even worse.''

''You tried it, huh?''

''I did,'' Longarm said. ''Dr. Marston will give you some medicine that will help. But mostly, it will just take a lot of time.''

''As long as it does heal and these headaches go away, I can wait it out.''

''Good!''

Longarm left the kid and decided to ride directly out to the Bar S Ranch and poke around. Maybe he'd find something useful, but he doubted it.

Chapter 15

It didn't take Longarm very long to check out the Bar S Ranch and see that any evidence that might have existed had already been obliterated by curiosity seekers and a sloppy undertaker. Longarm walked around for about twenty minutes, followed by a hard-faced and unfriendly-looking man who called himself George.

"I told you there was nothing left to see," the man growled as Longarm untied the reins from his horse. "Everyone in South Park came flockin' in here to see the bodies and offer their two bits worth on what must have happened."

"I understand that Red died hard."

"Shot in the belly, then the head," George said, spitting tobacco. "We figure that he had to have taken the gut slug first. He'd have suffered something awful, of course. Finally, the killer must have gotten bored and just put poor old Red out of his misery."

"And the other dead man they found?"

"Died of a broken neck."

"What do you think happened to the woman?"

"You mean Betty?"

"Yeah."

"I think she was taken against her will. I figure whoever killed Red took Betty for pleasure. She was one
hell of a good-lookin' gal."

"Maybe she'll try to kill him," Longarm suggested.

"Maybe. Betty isn't a full-blooded Ute, you know.
Her father was a Mexican. She's got a lot of fire, if you
understand what I mean."

"Did they ride off together?"

"Nope. Took Red's buggy and hitched a couple of
saddle horses to the back of it."

This was important news to Longarm. "Are you
sure?"

"Of course I am! The buggy was gone and it was the
only decent thing on four wheels that Red owned. He
and Betty used it all the time. You'd see 'em riding
around the valley every damned Sunday. It's black with
a red fringed top. Stands out so you can't miss it."

"Thanks," Longarm said, mounting Splash.

"You look more like an outlaw than a lawman,"
George said. "You look mean."

"I *am*," Longarm replied. "You have to be mean in
my business to stay alive."

"You damn sure better find the sonofabitch that gut-
shot, then executed Red and took Betty."

"I'll do my best," Longarm said. "I think they went
after the Marble brothers, or maybe another member of
their gang named Jake Mill."

George blinked, then said, "Jake was gunned down
in Cortez a few weeks ago."

"Is that right?"

"For a fact! He was ambushed. He was a hell of a fine man, you know. Tough sonofabitch too."

"Is that right?"

"It is."

"What about the Marble brothers?"

"They're also right handy with their guns. But Jake was the best of the bunch."

"Do you know *exactly* where I can find the brothers?"

"They keep on the move."

"Well," Longarm said, starting to rein away, "maybe I'll see you around. I'll be passing through Cortez and asking about Jake Mill."

"No need for that, Marshal. I told you he's dead."

"I have to make sure. Someone must have buried him and I need that information for my investigation. I'll be seeing you around, George."

"I doubt it."

Longarm frowned. "Why?"

"Either the Marble brothers or whoever the hell gut-shot Red will kill you first."

"I wouldn't bet on that," Longarm said. "A lot of men have tried, and a lot of men have died."

"Jake would have killed you for sure, Marshal. Nothin' he liked better than to kill some sonofabitchin' lawman."

"Well, then, I'm glad he was killed for that just saves me the trouble," Longarm said as he reined his horse around and started to ride off.

Longarm hadn't ridden twenty feet when he heard George curse. Instinctively, Longarm threw himself from Splash as George opened fire. Striking the ground, Longarm rolled over twice, dragging his own gun up and firing. His bullets struck George in the chest.

The man folded to his knees trying to raise his weapon and fire again.

Longarm hurried over to George and saw that the man was dying. "Who are you *really*?"

"Go to hell!"

"You're Jake Mill, aren't you?"

Jake's eyes burned with hatred but he locked his teeth, unwilling to cooperate.

"Well," Longarm said, "I guess that Jake Mill wasn't such a top gunman after all. In fact, you were piss-poor, in my professional opinion."

Jake choked with rage. "Tom and Dave will get you! Your luck can't last forever!"

Longarm collected the man's gun. "Luck had absolutely nothing to do with me beating you to the draw. I knew you were a damned outlaw."

"How!"

"This gun. You've cut notches on its handle. Pretty stupid thing to do, Jake. Besides that, you're wanted for murder and I had your description. I wasn't sure it was you until you began to brag about how good Jake Mill was with a gun. After that, there was no doubt in my mind."

"But . . . but you turned your back to me!"

"Yeah," Longarm said, "but I was making my play knowing that you would be taking your time thinking you could drill me. So you see, I had you figured out right from the start and you never really had a chance."

The outlaw tried to curse, but instead began to cough up blood. Longarm went back to his horse and remounted. Jake was almost gone, and Longarm figured that someone would eventually come along to bury the sorry, backshooting bastard.

•   •   •

Longarm pushed his horse hard, and arrived in Durango three days later. He and Splash were tired and hungry, so he wasted no time in getting the paint into a good livery and himself into the best hotel in town. He had a bath, a shave, and a steak in that order. When he stepped out of the cafe, the sun had gone down and Longarm was feeling human again. Human enough to even go in search of a couple of whiskeys and maybe a low-stakes game of monte or poker.

There was another reason why he thought it would be a good idea to socialize, and that was to ask questions about the Marble brothers. Longarm's information said that they wouldn't be in Durango, but one could never be certain. This was their backyard, and people in these parts could be expected to know of their comings and goings.

Longarm knocked the trail dust off his coat and went out to socialize. Durango was a pretty little town, but it wasn't all that big. He stopped at a saloon named the Flying Beaver and ordered a whiskey.

"Nice town," he said with a smile to the bartender.

"We like it."

"So do I. You lived here long?"

"About twenty years," the bartender said, not acting all that friendly. "Drinks are four bits each."

"Here," Longarm said, paying the man and leaving him an extra dime. "And here's to your good health!"

Longarm's hearty salute didn't even raise a smile out of the taciturn bartender, but he wasn't ready to quit yet. "Nice saloon. I like the way you've got it fixed up with all the animal heads mounted on the walls and this fine mahogany bar. Yes, sir, this is a real fine little establishment."

Instead of being flattered and pleased like any normal

human being, the bartender just growled, "You wanna buy the gawdamn joint? Sell 'er to you cheap."

"Sorry, but I'm not interested."

"Then who cares about what you think the place looks like?" the bartender snapped as he marched off to serve his regulars at the other end of the bar.

"Grouchy sonofabitch," Longarm muttered, finishing his whiskey and heading for the door without so much as even a wave of farewell.

The Square Peg Saloon looked to be a friendlier and much busier watering hole. Longarm went inside and had to wait a few moments in order to shoulder his way up against the bar and hail a bartender, who called, "What'll it be, stranger?"

"Whiskey!"

"Imported and in a bottle . . . or homegrown and served out of a mason jar?"

"Imported."

"Coming right up!"

Longarm thought the bartender was kidding about the homegrown whiskey until he saw him refilling another man's glass from a big mason jar.

"Four bits of a shot of Old Respectable, a fine brand of whiskey if I do say so myself," the bartender said to Longarm, arriving with an impressive-looking green bottle.

"Thanks," Longarm said. "Have you lived in this part of the country long?"

"Not nearly as long as I hope to," the bartender said, hurrying away.

Longarm turned to his right and looked into the glassy eyes of a drunkard who was clinging to the edge of the bar and swaying as if he were bracing himself against a high wind.

"Howdy," the man said with a lopsided grin. "Wanna buy me another drink?"

"No," Longarm replied, taking his whiskey and moving down the bar in search of someone who might give him a few leads on the Marble brothers.

He spotted an opening at the bar and eased up to a reasonably sober-looking cowboy. "How you doin'?" Longarm asked.

"I'm lookin' for a pretty gal named Alice and not seein' her right now," the cowboy said, craning his head all around. "That's how I'm doin'."

"I see some gals over there," Longarm said, pointing them out to the cowboy.

"Them's *new* whores to town and they want more money than I got left. Besides, I am crazy about Alice. But she's probably with some other fella."

"I suppose," Longarm said. "You happen to know either Dave or Joe Marble?"

The cowboy finally looked at Longarm. "Of course. Everyone knows 'em."

"You seen them in town lately?"

"Nope, but then, I ain't been in town much myself. Just got paid and now I can't even poke Alice until someone else has had his fill of her."

"Do the Marble brothers live around here?"

"Naw, they sold their place a couple years ago and they keep on the move." The cowboy regarded Longarm closely. "Why you askin' about them boys?"

"They owe me."

"Well, you ain't likely to collect anything but a damned bullet."

"They're pretty tough, huh?"

"Yep, and as techy as teased snakes."

"I see. Maybe they're in Cortez."

147

"Probably," the cowboy said. "I heard that's the last place they were spotted."

"How long ago?"

"About two weeks. Last I heard, they were rustlin' cattle again. Mostly, though, they rob banks and stage-coaches. Them boys are good at it and always have a lot of money."

"I see." Longarm tossed down his drink and ordered one for the cowboy and another for himself. He and the cowboy talked awhile more, but then Alice appeared and the cowboy jumped up and disappeared.

Longarm finished his drink and played a few hands of poker, hoping to learn more about the comings and goings of the Marble brothers. But no one at the card table was in a mind for loose talk, so Longarm quit the game and went up to his room and went to bed.

He awoke the next morning to the sound of a battle going on between a screaming woman and some man who was giving her a hard time. Longarm dragged himself out of his bed, stretched, and reached for his six-gun. He heard the woman hit the hallway floor, and then heard her cry of pain cut short.

Longarm jumped to the door and unbolted it, then stepped outside to see that there were *two* very big and very drunk men standing over a young woman that he recognized as Alice.

"Step back!" Longarm ordered.

"You better mind your own business!" one of them ordered.

Longarm cracked the man across the bridge of his nose with the barrel of his gun. The man reeled away in pain, and the other fella made a play for his holstered gun and also got pistol-whipped for his stupidity.

"Now get out of here before I shoot you both!" Longarm shouted at the retreating pair.

When they were gone, Longarm helped Alice to her feet. She was disheveled and had a nasty bruise across one side of her face, but was otherwise in pretty good shape.

"You're a little small to be taking on a pair like that, aren't you?" Longarm asked.

"I thought better of them," Alice replied. "I don't usually make that bad a mistake."

"Well, I hope not," Longarm told her, "or you could wind up dead the next time."

"Who are you?"

"Custis. And your name is Alice."

"How'd you know that?"

"An admirer of yours told me," Longarm explained. "I didn't catch his name but he was a lovesick cowboy."

"That would have been Monte. For some fool reason, he keeps asking me to marry him—even when he's sober!"

"Maybe you should marry the man. He seems like a fine fella and he adores you, Alice."

"But he's a cowboy. I can't go out and live in some line shack while he nursemaids a bunch of cows. Uh-uh, that's not the life for me."

"Maybe he'd change his line of work and get a town job."

"Maybe," Alice said, looking doubtful. "But I'm not too sure that he'd be very happy living in town."

"Yeah," Longarm said, "but I can't imagine you're very happy now either."

"You got that right. Say, mister, would you mind if I use your room to clean up a little?"

"Not at all," Longarm said, leading the way.

He stretched out on the bed and watched as Alice used his washbasin to freshen up. She opened a small handbag and applied some makeup in order to partially hide her fresh and angry bruises.

"How old are you?" Longarm blurted out.

"Old enough to know better than to take on two ornery sonofabitches at once."

"Marry Monte," Longarm urged. "Then start over fresh."

She turned and really looked at him. "You don't *look* like no preacher but you sure *sound* like one."

"I'm a United States deputy marshal."

"You are!"

"Yes."

"Lemme see a badge."

Longarm dug his badge out of his coat, causing Alice to cluck her tongue with surprise. "Well, no wonder you took care of them two sonofabitches the way you did! Why didn't you arrest and throw them in jail for beating me up?"

"I'm after bigger prey," Longarm explained. "And I really would appreciate it if you would not tell anyone that I'm a marshal."

"Sure, if that's the way you want it."

"It is."

"Who are you after, Marshal?"

"Joe and Dave Marble. Do you know anything about them that might help me?"

To Longarm's surprise, Alice laughed outright. "Why, I know the size of their peckers! And I know that Dave's is longer than his brother's, who grunts like a pig when he's coupling. Tom is slow, but sometimes he gets too drunk to get it up, and once he even fell asleep while I was undressing! Can you imagine?''

"Not hardly," Longarm said, "but I need to know how to find them."

"They're in Cortez."

"Are you sure?"

"Pretty sure," Alice said. "The word is that they stole some cattle and are peddling them off a few at a time."

"Thanks," Longarm said, collecting his gear as he prepared to take up the outlaw trail again.

"Hey, Marshal. I owe you for this. You want a little fun this morning?"

"No, thanks."

Alice blinked with surprise. "I know I look a little rough, but I can make you howl like a lobo wolf."

"Uh-uh."

"Why not?"

" 'Cause I'm betting that you are smart enough to marry Monte the next time he comes to town."

Alice, despite her bruises and pains, put her hands on her shapely hips and laughed. "Why, I do believe you are the *strangest* marshal I ever met. All the others either wanted to arrest or hump me, one or the other."

"Get out of here," Longarm said with an easy grin. "I've seen a lot of pretty young girls like you, and the ones that keep whoring all wind up either dead or diseased. It's no life for any woman, Alice. You're smart enough to figure that out for yourself."

"Well," she said, going over to the door, "Monte did say that his parents have a little spread over in Arizona. He told me that we could get married and they'd let us build a cabin and give us some cattle to start a herd."

"Sounds good. Did he say where the ranch was?"

"Near a town called Prescott."

"One of my favorite parts of Arizona," Longarm said. "Marry the kid and go there. Let him raise cattle and you start raising children and see how good life can be, Alice."

She shook her head and sighed. "Gawdamn, Marshal, I think I've plumb figured you out at last."

"Is that right?"

"Yep. You're a romantic. That's *exactly* what you are. A romantic. I bet anything that you can even spout a sonnet or two, can't ya?"

Longarm blushed, and then he shooed Alice out the door before he started thinking about getting romantic with her himself. Once those bruises healed and she started living clean and getting her rest, that girl was going to be beautiful.

Ten minutes later, Longarm was striding into the livery.

"Why, you look like a new man!" the owner exclaimed with a wide grin.

"How is Splash?"

"I've curried him to a shine and grained him. I'd say he's ready to ride."

"Thanks," Longarm said, paying the man and saddling the paint himself. "How long will it take me to reach Cortez?"

"You'll be there by sundown, if not sooner."

"They got a hotel and a livery?"

"Yep, but none as good as mine."

"I'll be back through," Longarm promised.

"Marshal, you be careful when you brace the Marble brothers," the liveryman said, looking concerned. "They're real bad."

"How'd you know that I was a marshal and that I was after the Marble brothers?"

"Everyone in town knows it. Why else would you have been asking about 'em last night?"

"Yeah," Longarm said drily, "why else? By the way, did you happen to see a carriage pass through town with a couple of horses in tow?"

"There are a lot of 'em passin' through Durango every day."

"This one was real nice with a black top and red fringe."

"By jingo, I *did* see that buggy. Was a man and a real pretty Indian girl at his side."

"I think she is his hostage."

"I doubt that," the liveryman said.

"Why?"

"She was all tight up against him with her arm linked around his waist. She looked real happy."

"Well I'll be . . ." Longarm didn't finish. Instead, he just tightened his cinch before he stepped into his saddle and headed off for Cortez.

Chapter 16

The Assassin was starting to have second thoughts about what was most important in his life. Before meeting Betty, the only thing that held any meaning was revenge. But now, after almost a week with this woman, he was ready to believe that he could again find happiness. That he might live for something more than to kill the last of the men who had caused the death of his wife and son. Revenge was sweet, but it was a sweet poison that starved rather than nourished the soul. The Assassin wondered if he might be able to fall in love once more. To have even considered this possibility a few weeks before would have been completely unimaginable.

It was a fine day to be alive. Since they had left Durango and headed west toward Cortez, the country had undergone a significant change. Now it was lower, more open, and the high mountain evergreens had been replaced by sage and pinyon as well as juniper. The air was warmer, the colors softer, browns and grays instead of dark greens.

"This looks like sheep country to me," Betty remarked. "Better sheep than cattle country."

"Do you know something about sheep?"

"I know a *lot* about sheep."

Smith was driving the buggy, and now he turned and looked at her with undisguised curiosity. "How?"

"My father was a sheepman. When I was a girl, we used to summer in the Sangre de Cristo Mountains and winter on the high New Mexican deserts. We were nomads. We owned no land, only many thousands of sheep."

"Did your father prosper?"

"For a time. But he didn't realize that greedy cattlemen would fence the lands so that we could not move our flocks between the summer and winter ranges. In time, there was no place to go except to the worst of the desert. For this reason, our sheep began to starve. We had to almost give them away one winter. That was the year that my father got drunk and shot a rancher who had fenced off his last passageway to the high mountains and our last hope for summer range."

"He *shot* the rancher?"

"Yes, and killed him."

"Then what happened?"

"My father and mother fled to Mexico, but they were caught and hanged."

"Why did they hang your mother?"

"Because," Betty said, "she and my father put up a fight and killed a couple more gringos just north of El Paso."

"Where were you when all this was happening?"

"In Taos with my Aunt Monica. She was ill and I loved her very much."

Smith shook his head. "It sounds like a tragic time for you. Did your aunt at least recover?"

"No. She died that same winter."

"How old were you?"

"Fourteen."

"And what happened then?"

"I went to work in a cantina," Betty said, her eyes clouding with sadness. "I worked there several years. I . . . I had many men, some good but most bad. And I lost a baby. I almost died, and then Red found me and took me to the Bar S, where I have lived ever since."

"Were you really happy living with him?"

"Sometimes yes, sometimes no," Betty said after a long pause. "You see, Red Skoal was mostly nice to me. He saved my life, but I knew that he was an outlaw and had killed many men. And sometimes, when he drank too much, he was very rough with me, but he was always sorry the next morning."

"And you don't blame me for killing him?"

"No, because he was one of the men that killed your family. He told me about that, you know."

"I don't want to hear of it," Smith said, shaking his head back and forth. "Not ever."

She kissed his pale cheek. "I will never speak of that or of Red again. You have my word of honor."

"Thank you," he said quietly. "And I promise I will treat you with kindness."

"Maybe that is not enough for me now. Eh?"

Smith knew what she wanted to hear, and he said, "All right, I love you, Betty. I will always love you."

"And be faithful?"

"Yes."

"And even marry me?"

He glanced sideways at her with a big smile. "Of course. It would make me very proud to have you for my wife."

Betty radiated happiness. "Maybe I can even give you another fine son."

Smith opened his mouth to tell her that he did not want another son. That it was all his heart could stand to risk loving another woman. But when he looked very deep into Betty's eyes, he knew he could not tell her this because she very much wanted a son of her own. So he nodded in agreement and pretended not to notice when she wiped away her tears.

Cortez was a burgeoning livestock center where one was as likely to meet outlaws as cowboys or Indians. The Navajo and Hopi peoples mixed and traded freely with whites and Mexicans, and the architecture of the town was a mix of frontier shanty and old Santa Fe adobe. When Jim Smith and Betty drove up the center of town, they hardly attracted a glance because the townspeople were accustomed to seeing a lot of passing strangers.

"I'm not going to waste any time in asking for their whereabouts," Smith announced. "My experience is that the news of our arrival will travel fast. The best thing to do is to find the Marble brothers before they even know we're looking for them."

"They might be watching us right now," Betty said nervously. "They know that I was Red's woman."

"Well," Smith replied matter-of-factly, "that can't be helped. Let's just hope we see them before they see us."

Smith left his team at a livery and collected their few traveling bags. After getting directions to a suitable hotel, he said, "We're old friends of Tom and Dave Marble. Would you happen to know if they're in town?"

"I saw Dave yesterday," the liveryman announced. "But not Tom. I heard that they've had a little parting of the ways."

"Oh?"

"You see, Dave got drunk and cut Tom's cinch almost clean away as a practical joke. When Tom started to gallop out of town, his cinch broke and he took a real bad spill. Nearly broke his neck."

"Some practical joke."

"Yeah," the liveryman agreed with a shake of his head. "Anyway, it knocked Tom out cold and everyone hoped he was dead. But he wasn't. And when he came around and learned that his own brother had cut his cinch, they had a real donnybrook. Fought up and down the street and tore up the Medallion Saloon. Tom was always the toughest of the pair, and he just beat the living hell out of Dave. Then he took Dave's good cinch to replace his own and galloped out of town."

"Where did he go?" Smith asked.

"Out to their place about ten miles west of town, I reckon," the liveryman said. "I ain't seen their spread, but I hear it has a cabin and a good spring. He and some Indian are huntin' wild horses. I've bought a few of 'em myself. Pretty good animals, for mustangs."

"Where is Dave right now?" Betty asked.

"My guess he's drinkin' and playin' cards back at the Medallion Saloon. That's his usual hangout."

Smith pivoted to gaze down the street. "That the one?" he asked, pointing.

"Yep. But there's no ladies allowed inside," the liveryman said, eyes coming to rest on Betty. "Just whores, ma'am."

"Thanks," Betty replied as she took Smith's arm and they started down the street.

"You're not going in there," Smith told her. "We're getting a room at the hotel and you'll wait there until this killing business is finally finished."

"But . . ."

"Don't argue with me," Smith told her in a firm, but quiet voice. "If you were with me when I braced Dave Marble, I'd be thinking about you maybe taking a stray bullet instead of how I needed to drop Dave in his tracks. You could be my fatal distraction."

"All right then," she said as they approached the recommended hotel.

They had a room in less than ten minutes, and then Smith said a quick good-bye. "Betty, don't you worry. I'll be back before you know it."

"Dave is very cunning, very dangerous," she warned, following him out into the hallway. "You don't give him any chance at all or he will think of some way to kill you."

"All right," Smith called back over his shoulder as he hurried down the hall.

The Medallion Saloon was a pigpen with a filthy sawdust floor, cobwebs in the rafters, and a rough-looking crowd of heavy drinkers. Smith supposed he had seen the interior of worse-looking saloons, but they were beyond his immediate recollection.

He quickly spotted Dave Marble, although he might have missed identifying him if he hadn't been told by the liveryman about how Dave had been beaten by his brother. Dave's face was dark with angry bruises and his fist-busted lips were black smears of crusty scabs. One of Dave's eyes was almost swollen shut and he looked as if he ought to be in a hospital instead of a saloon. The man was seated at the rearmost table with his back to the wall. He was surrounded by four other men, and although there was a deck of cards on the table, they weren't playing.

Smith wondered if he should try to lure Dave away from his friends, then decided to hell with it. The urge for revenge was so strong in him that nothing would do except to walk right up to the outlaw and force a showdown.

"You're Dave Marble," he said, coming to a halt before the table.

"That's right," Marble said, looking up. "What of it?"

"You and your gang set fire to my house in Denver and killed my wife and son. Now I'm going to kill *you*."

Marble had been slouched down in his chair, but now he straightened up in a hurry, raising his hands and saying, "Whoa, there, stranger! When did this awful thing happen?"

"A few months ago."

"In Denver, you say?"

"That's right."

"I ain't *been* in Denver for almost two years!"

"Stand up," Smith rasped, hand shadowing the butt of his sixgun.

"Now wait a damn minute here!" Dave shouted. "You got the wrong damned man!"

"No I haven't," Smith assured him with a cold grin. "I already killed Skoal and Trabert, and now I'm going to kill *you*!"

Dave gulped and developed a twitch at the left corner of his mouth. "Now . . . now I don't know who you are, mister, but you've got no quarrel with me. I tell you, I

161

haven't been to Denver in two years. You got the wrong man.''

"Stand up and make your play, or take a bullet sitting down," Smith commanded, ignoring the protests. "Either way is the same to me."

Dave threw up his hands. "If you kill me, it'll be murder and you'll hang! Ain't that right, boys?''

His companions nervously nodded their heads.

"For the last time," Smith ordered, "stand up and fight!''

Dave jumped up, heaving the table away from himself into Smith and diving for cover as he reached for his six-gun. The heavy table struck Smith in the groin, knocking him off balance. Before he could recover, a shot rang out and Smith felt a searing fire explode against his shoulder. He went reeling backward and then crashed over another table. His gun spilled from his hand and his head struck the dirty sawdust floor. Smith knew that he was about to become a dead man.

Dave Marble jumped forward, smoking gun clenched in his big hand. "You sonofabitch! Did you *really* get lucky enough to kill my friends?''

"Damn right!" Smith choked.

"You're going to die real slow," Dave said, raising his six-gun and taking aim at Smith's knee. "I've got five bullets left in this gun and you're going to feel every damn one of them."

Smith tried to kick out and knock Dave over, but the man was smart enough to stay out of reach. He laughed scornfully at Smith's feeble effort and again took careful aim.

The Winchester clenched in Betty's fists boomed and caused Dave Marble to take an exaggerated goose step backward. His chin dropped to his shirt and he stared down at the hole in his chest as a bright crimson trickle of blood sprang from his mouth. Then, with his legs beginning to buckle, he looked up and stared at the woman standing in the doorway.

"Betty?" he croaked, trying hard to focus.

"That's right."

"But . . . why!"

"Because you deserve death!" she cried, levering another shell into the rifle and sending it scorching through his brain.

Betty rushed inside the saloon. Pointing her rifle at the most harmless-looking pair she could find, she yelled, "You and you, pick my friend up and bring him with me!"

A half hour later, a doctor left their hotel room, saying, "I'll have to dig that slug out first thing tomorrow morning if you ain't dead before then."

"I won't be," Smith vowed.

"Just don't move or you'll start bleeding again!"

When they were alone, Betty said, "What are we going to do about Tom?"

"I'll kill him too," Smith promised.

"No, we'll do it *together*," she said. "That way, I know you will not be shot again."

"I should have just shot Dave instead of giving him an explanation," Smith said angrily. "That was my big mistake tonight."

"*We* will have to do better with Tom, or he will kill us for sure," Betty said, coming to lie down beside him.

"I guess you're right," Smith agreed, using his good arm to draw her close. "A whole hell of lot better."

"I'm glad you finally are making sense," Betty whispered, kissing his pale cheek.

Chapter 17

It was late afternoon when Longarm galloped into the little Colorado ranching town of Cortez, and the saloons were already doing a brisk business. Longarm tied Splash in front of one called the Two Bits Bar and wearily strode inside. No one seemed to pay him the slightest bit of attention, and he ordered a whiskey and drank it down neat.

"Bartender?"

"You want another?"

"Yeah," Longarm said, "but first I need some information."

The bartender was in his thirties, a handsome man with his oily black hair parted down the middle and a dimple in each cheek. He leaned close across the bar and said with a smile, "Information might cost you more than my whiskey, stranger."

"I'm looking for a man with burn marks on his neck who is traveling with a pretty woman that looks to be either Indian or Mexican. They would have hit this town driving a buggy. Black with red fringe on top.''

The bartender poured Longarm another shot. "Whiskey is two bits a throw, information one dollar.''

"Fair enough,'' Longarm said, paying the man.

"The pair you describe,'' the bartender said, after refilling Longarm's glass, "is holed up at the Fairplay Hotel just down the street.''

"Are you sure?''

"Yep. Fact is, that couple is famous in this town. Are you a friend of the Marble brothers?''

"No, but why do you ask?''

"Because the man braced Dave Marble but had the tables turned on him and was shot.''

"The Assassin was shot!''

The bartender frowned. "The Assassin? Is that what he is called?''

"By some, yes. Anyway,'' Longarm said impatiently, "what happened then?''

"Well, that woman he was with came in and shot Dave Marble down with a rifle. Just drilled him twice as clean as you please.''

"She did?''

"I'm tellin' you the truth.'' The bartender straightened up and glanced down his bar. "Hey, boys, didn't that pretty Indian gal kill Dave Marble last night?''

"Damn right!'' a bearded man shouted. "Shot him deader than a doornail!''

The other patrons nodded in agreement, and one yelled, "Let's have a toast for the Indian gal who did us all a big favor!''

Longarm raised his own glass and joined the toast. He was now a believer. Then he said, "And what happened to the couple after that?''

"The man was wounded in the shoulder," the bartender said. "Our Doc Halsey dug the bullet out early this morning. The fella is in rough shape, but he's expected to live."

"And the woman?"

"She's stickin' to her man like a louse on a tall dog," the bartender answered. "People around here are betting that Tom Marble is going to learn of this and come to kill 'em both, but until then, they're famous."

"We ought to help them two get away," an old man with tobacco-stained whiskers interjected. "We ought to put 'em in their buggy and send 'em packin!"

"Sure," another said sarcastically. "Then Tom will shoot up the town and probably kill a couple of us for our trouble. Uh-uh, I say it's not our fight."

"You chicken-shit sonofabitch!" the old man rasped. "You ain't got the balls of a piss-ant!"

The insulted man made a lunge for the old codger, but Longarm stepped between the squabbling pair. "That's enough of that," he growled.

"Why you want to know about those two?" the bartender asked, pouring himself a shot of whiskey. "I mean, if you don't mind my asking."

"I *do* mind," Longarm said, unable to see any advantage to be gained by tipping his hand or revealing his true identity. "Anyway, point me to the Fairplay Hotel."

"Can't miss it," the old man said. "Just six or seven doors down to your right."

The Fairplay Hotel was clearly one of the town's nicer establishments. It was clean and had decent furniture in its small but tasteful lobby. A desk clerk glanced up from a dime novel that he had been reading and managed a smile.

"Afternoon," he said. "Care for a room?"

"Maybe later," Longarm replied. "Right now, I've come to visit some folks."

"Are they expecting you?" the clerk asked.

"I'm looking for a man named Jim Smith. He's with a woman named Betty."

"Can't say I know them."

Longarm marched up to the desk and leaned on it for a moment saying, "If you don't tell me what room they are in and give me a key to their door, I'll have to break down every room in the house and rouse *all* your customers. It'll be a lot worse that way."

"Oh."

"Give me the key," Longarm ordered, reaching into his pocket and showing the man his badge. "And do it now."

"Yes, sir!" the desk clerk snapped, jumping for a board where every room's extra key was affixed to a separate hook. "Room Six! Just to your left."

"Thanks."

"You gonna shoot them?" the desk clerk asked. "I sure hope you don't have to kill 'em. They're real nice and they did this town a big favor when they gunned down Dave Marble. Marshal, I . . ."

Longarm wasn't listening. The hunt was about to end. He'd been tracking The Assassin for weeks now, always coming upon the aftermath of his destruction. That was not to say that each man Smith had killed didn't deserve to die, not at all. In fact, The Assassin had saved the taxpayers a fair amount of time and expense. But he was a murderer himself and now he was about to be brought to justice.

Longarm placed his ear to the door of Room Number Six and listened. He couldn't hear a thing, and didn't see any light shining under the doorjamb, so he gathered that either the couple was sleeping, or they had made their escape unbeknownst to the clerk or anyone else in Cortez.

Longarm turned and tiptoed back to the desk. "When was the last time you saw them?"

"They sent out for some food and I brought it to their room a couple of hours ago. The man was pale, but he was sitting up in bed with his shoulder all bandaged. He smiled and even tipped me for my trouble. The woman said thank you."

"Is there a window in that room?"

"Of course! All our rooms have windows."

"Opening upon what?"

"Room Six has a window facing out in back with an excellent view of the mountains. Nice view of the mountains. In fact, they complimented me on the room and I said that I . . ."

Again, Longarm cut the conversation short by turning away and heading up the hall. But this time, when he came to Room Number Six, he slipped the key into the lock and gently turned it until he heard a faint click.

"Marshal?"

Longarm had been just about to open the door and rush inside when the clerk tapped him on the shoulder.

"Get out of here!" Longarm snapped in a hushed voice. "And don't come back! There could be bullets flying!"

The desk clerk retreated back up the hallway, and Longarm returned his attention to the door. Squeezing the knob in one hand and lifting his gun from his holster, he took a deep breath and pushed the door open, stepping quickly inside.

It was dark, but he could see a man in bed with a

bulky white bandage taped to his shoulder. The man smiled and said, "It's too dim in here to see your face, but are you Tom Marble?"

"No, I'm Deputy Marshal Custis Long from Denver and you are under arrest for murder."

"I see. Well, you do understand my motives, don't you?"

"Yes, but that doesn't excuse them and you're still under arrest."

"I'm wounded."

"So I've heard," Longarm said, keeping his gun up. "Where is Betty?"

"Right here," she replied, stepping in from behind the door and shoving a gun into Longarm's ribs. "Drop it, Marshal Long, or so help me God I will kill you!"

Longarm knew that she wasn't bluffing. Betty had shot down Dave Marble, and she wouldn't hesitate to do the same thing to him.

"You're making a big mistake, miss. Up until right now, you've done nothing that a little jail time wouldn't fix. But this is obstruction of justice and—"

"You talk too much," Betty hissed, prodding his ribs even harder. "Drop your gun or I'll kill you!"

Longarm dropped his gun.

"Over against the wall with your hands up," Betty ordered as she shut the door and bolted it behind her.

Smith lit the bedside lamp, and now Longarm got a very good look at The Assassin. Without the bandanna wrapped around his neck, you could clearly see the red, proud flesh, and Longarm was sure that there was a lot more of it covered by the blankets.

"Betty," Smith said, dragging his own gun out from under the blankets, "frisk Marshal Long for any hidden weapons. Be very careful because I have heard that he carries a hideout derringer.''

Betty kept her gun in her hand as she frisked Longarm, discovering the derringer attached to his watch chain. She also found a knife in his boot top that he had taken to wearing during some of his manhunts after once desperately needing one to save his life.

"Anything else?" Smith asked.

"Not unless he's got it stuffed up his butt," Betty said, stepping away with her gun still trained on Longarm.

"Sit down on the floor, Marshal," Smith ordered. "I've heard a great deal about you but we've never really met, have we?"

"No."

"What are they saying about me back in Denver?"

"That you became a rogue killer. That you murdered Commissioner John Pinter by shoving him off the Federal Building's rooftop."

"Wrong!" Smith exploded. "Your mighty commissioner jumped off the roof because he was so damned deep in debt to the criminals there that they were about to blow the whistle on him. If they had, he'd have lost everything, including the respect and love of his dear wife.''

"Can you prove that?"

"All you have to do is return to Denver and dig up some of the dirt. You can start by asking a very unsavory fellow named Dude Conley. He's the one that Pinter owed the most money to. But there were plenty of others, and they were all coming after your hallowed commissioner. He was finished and knew it. They would have destroyed his reputation, not to mention breaking his neck. So he took the easy way out and jumped off the roof.''

''Give me a few more names of the men he owed money to.''

''Don Prater. Sid Lowry. Big Mo Brown and Ronnie the Bull. You *must* have heard of them.''

''I've put some of them in jail.''

''Yeah, well, they're all out now and they're making an excellent living off people like your commissioner, Marshal.''

Smith beckoned the woman over to his bedside, and then took her hand in his own and squeezed it tight. ''Back in Denver I was making your commissioner look very, very good. Crime was down and he was getting talked about as a likely candidate for a high political office.''

Longarm listened without comment for nearly an hour until he was confident that he was hearing the truth. That indeed Commissioner John Pinter, a handsome and congenial figure known in Denver society, had been a secret gambler and had lost his soul to the city's criminal element. It was not so uncommon, and every one of the men that Smith had named were known to be high-stakes gamblers and extortionists.

''Even if what you are telling me is true,'' Longarm said, ''that doesn't change the fact that you are guilty of murder. No one but the courts has the authority to judge and then execute the guilty.''

''They murdered my wife and child!'' Smith screamed. ''*That* gave me the authority!''

Longarm looked away. He suddenly found himself very sympathetic to this man, even though he knew Smith possessed a very dark and murderous side to his complex personality. But then again . . .

"I just want to kill Tom Marble," Smith told him. "And then Jake Mill."

"Jake Mill's dead," said Longarm. "I shot him at Red Skoal's ranch."

Smith looked surprised, then relieved. "Then that leaves Tom Marble, He's the last and the worst."

"And after you kill him?"

"Then I want to be left alone. I want to take Betty and become a . . . a shop owner or something equally as boring. I don't ever want to hurt, much less kill, anyone again."

"So what do we do now?"

Smith glanced at Betty, as if hoping for an answer. She looked away. "All right," Smith said, "we'll take you with us to find Tom Marble. But *I'll* kill him, not you."

"And then?" Longarm asked. "What are you going to do, kill me as well?"

"No!" Smith lowered his voice. "We'll turn you loose somewhere out in the hills where you can't get to a horse or any help for a few days. And during that time, maybe you'll come to your senses and decide that I deserve absolution. That Betty and I deserve the chance to start over with a new life. I'm asking for nothing more than that. No medals or money for the scum I've rid the people of Colorado of. Just freedom and . . . justice."

"I'm not a judge," Longarm said quietly. "It's not up to me to exonerate someone from the kinds of crimes that you have committed for revenge."

"Sure," Smith said, bitterness thick in his voice. "You're just another lawman going by the book. Following the rules without exception. Right or wrong. Black or white. Guilty . . . or innocent. Is that it, Marshal Long? Have I pegged you correctly?"

"When," Longarm asked, pointedly ignoring the question, "are we leaving to get Tom Marble?"

"Why not tomorrow morning? I'll be much stronger by then."

"Suits me," Longarm replied.

"Turn around," Smith ordered. "We'll tie you up overnight. We'll have supper brought in tonight, and tomorrow morning, after we have breakfast, we'll ride out and settle this thing once and for all."

"All right," Longarm said, turning around and putting his hands behind his back. "You're the man holding the winning hand this round."

"That's right," Smith said. "And don't you forget it. Up to now, I've never killed anyone that didn't need killing. Don't force me to make you the exception."

"I wouldn't dream of it," Longarm growled, feeling rope bite into his bare wrists.

Chapter 18

Surprisingly, they all slept well that night. Longarm was allowed to sleep in an overstuffed chair, but only after his ankles had been tied securely to its legs so that he could not possibly have attacked his slumbering captors without making enough noise to awaken them. And after a good breakfast in the room, Longarm's ankles were untied and he was led up the street to collect poor Splash, who had not been fed or watered. Longarm complained about the mistreatment of his mount.

"It'll take a while for the liveryman to get the buggy hitched," Smith reasoned. "In the meantime, you can water and grain your paint horse, but Betty will have you under her gun at all times."

"Thanks," Longarm said drily.

The townspeople watched but did not interfere, which did not surprise Longarm. Maybe they knew he was a United States marshal, but they also knew that Smith and Betty had rid them of Dave Marble and were planning to kill his even more hated and dangerous brother, Tom.

As the three were leaving town with Longarm's wrists tied in front of him, Longarm said, "A bartender told me that Tom Marble was staying just outside—"

"We already know where he's staying," Betty interrupted. "And we know that he is not alone."

"Then maybe," Longarm said, his patience wearing razor-blade thin, "you two vigilantes ought to at least consider letting me help you!"

"No, thanks," Smith said, looking amazingly chipper for a man with a fresh bullet hole in his shoulder.

Two hours later, they came in sight of the little spread where Tom Marble was supposedly staying. They drew up about a half mile from the ranch house and studied it for a long time.

"What are we going to do now?" Longarm finally asked. "Or were you just planning to drive in there and allow us to be shot down from ambush?"

For the first time, Smith appeared undecided. Longarm also noticed that the man was not looking so chipper anymore. In fact, he was very pale and in considerable pain. Longarm had a hunch that his bullet wound had reopened because of the jarring buggy ride and that the man was now losing more blood.

"I suppose we could wait and go in after dark," Smith gritted out, "but I'd like to get this over with as quickly as possible."

"Because you're fading fast," Longarm said. "Isn't that the truth? You're afraid that, if you wait, you'll be in no shape to kill Tom. In fact, you're afraid you might even bleed to death."

"Let's just go on in," Smith wheezed, ignoring Longarm and turning to Betty. "Tom will recognize you but

I doubt he'll recognize me. What about you, Marshal? Will he recognize you?''

"Not likely."

"Then let's just drive on in as bold as brass," Smith said, forcing the issue.

"Sure wish you'd untie my wrists and let me have my gun," Longarm told them. "If you are killed, I'm also as good as dead."

"Then you'd better hope we nail Tom before he nails us."

Longarm studied the distant house and the corrals. There were two saddled horses tied to a tree shading the house. "Whoever is there has already seen us," he said. "If we ride up to the cabin like this, they'll realize that my hands are tied and they'll shoot us down in cold blood."

"Maybe not," Smith said weakly.

"Dammit, man!" Longarm protested. "They'll kill *Betty* too! Tom Marble will soon learn that she killed his brother. And how do you think he'll react to that?"

"I . . . I don't know."

"Of course you do!"

"Don't listen to him," Betty warned, trying to take control of the reins and drive on. "I'll be all right."

But Smith knew better. "Wait a minute," he said quietly. "Betty, I'm afraid that the marshal is right this time. Tom *would* kill you."

"But not if we kill him first!"

"We can't take that chance," Smith reasoned. "I'm not in very good shape. I could get killed and then you'd be entirely at the mercy of that bloody-handed sonofabitch."

"But . . ."

"Untie our friend," Smith gently ordered. "But don't give him back his gun."

"Dammit!" Longarm protested. "What can I do to help without a gun!"

"I don't know. But given your reputation, you'll probably think of something."

Longarm wasn't happy, but at least now he'd have some chance of defending himself and the woman. He made another attempt to talk them into allowing him to have his gun back, but got nowhere.

"All right," he told them, "since you're not thinking too clearly, I suggest we wait until after dark. That way, they won't have a clear, long-range rifle shot at us."

Smith used his handkerchief to mop cold sweat from his brow. He was starting to shake with the chills. "I . . . I don't know," he muttered. "Betty, what do you think?"

"I think he's right," she replied, staring at the ranch house. "There are men are watching us. I can *feel* their eyes. They may even have looking glasses and have recognized me."

"Okay," Smith said, leaning his head back on the seat cushion and breathing heavily. "Let's wait until dark then."

"Mind if I dismount, hobble my horse, and let him graze while we wait?" Longarm asked.

But Smith had already dozed off into a fitful sleep.

"Sure," Betty finally said, examining her man's bandaged shoulder.

"Has the wound reopened?" Longarm asked.

"Yes."

"He might very well bleed to death," Longarm said. "He needs to get back to that doctor you found in Cortez."

Betty shook her head. "If we do not kill Tom here, then he will come to Cortez and kill *us*!"

"Not if you give me a gun and let me arrest him first." Longarm dismounted. "It's the right thing to do, Betty."

"No! You would put Jim in prison!"

"I think he'd get a fair trial and . . . if what he said about the commissioner is true and he really didn't kill him . . . well, he'd soon go free. Especially if I made the case that, when the chips were down, he acted responsibly and allowed me to finally do my duty."

"What about the other members of the gang that he has *already* killed?"

"Self-defense," Longarm told her. "You killed one of them too, remember? I'll write up the report saying that you had no choice but to kill Dave Marble. Trabert. Red Skoal. They're all cut from the same rotten bolt of cloth."

"How do I know you are not saying this just to trick me?"

"You're going to have to have a little faith," Longarm told the worried woman. "It's your call and you need to make the right one."

She pulled Smith's coat back and again gazed at the blood-soaked bandages. Longarm saw her bite her lower lip, and she was stiff with anxiety.

"I'm a man of my word," Longarm said quietly. "And I *can* arrest Tom Marble as well as anyone else waiting in that ranch house. Trust me."

"All right!" Betty jumped down from the buggy with a six-gun and rifle. She strode up to Longarm saying, "Here! Go and kill them all!"

"Not unless I have to," Longarm said, examining both weapons. "Betty, you did the right thing. And if I

179

should go down, you turn this buggy around and head for parts unknown. *Don't* go back to Cortez because Tom will follow you there.''

''I'm afraid that Jim is bleeding to death!'' she cried. ''And there is nothing I can do to stop it!''

Longarm went to examine the man. The wound was hemorrhaging and the inside lining of Smith's coat was soaked with fresh blood.

Longarm pulled off his own coat, then his shirt, which he tore into strips. ''Maybe I can cinch this thing down tight enough to stop the bleeding until we get back to the doctor.''

''We are grateful and . . . and I think that you *are* a good man.''

''Thanks,'' he said, knowing it might already be too late to save The Assassin's life. ''Let's just hope that I won't become a dead one.''

Longarm waited until sunset before he mounted Splash and started off to circle the ranch house. The pounding of his heart seemed much louder than the pounding of Splash's swiftly moving hooves.

When he came to within a hundred yards of the cabin, Longarm dismounted and hobbled the paint, then went the rest of the way on foot. He reached the back of the cabin and stopped to listen, but could hear nothing. Even so, he knew that Tom and at least one other man was waiting.

Longarm waited about a quarter of an hour, and then he slipped around to the front of the cabin. He picked up a rock that lay beside the foundation and hurled it at a rusting five-gallon milk can that lay discarded in the yard. He missed the can, but the rock skipped across the ground and slapped one of the tied horses, causing it to jump back and snap its reins.

A muzzle flash exploded from the cabin's doorway, and Longarm jumped out and fired almost point-blank. He heard a scream, and then another man jumped out shooting wildly. Longarm jumped behind a water trough and fired three rounds at the sprinting silhouette. He heard his slugs hit the man twice. The silhouette staggered badly and grunted in pain, and Longarm shouted, "Stop! I'm a United States deputy marshal and you are under arrest!"

In reply, the man twisted around and fired in Longarm's direction, narrowly missing him. Longarm returned fire as the man crawled into his saddle and began to flee. Taking careful aim this time, Longarm drilled the fugitive in the back. He watched the big silhouette lift up in his stirrups, then throw his hands high into the air. After that, the fugitive tumbled off his running horse and crashed to the ranch yard, where he lay still.

Longarm lit a match and hurried to the doorway of the cabin. The first man he'd killed was an Indian, probably the Navajo horse thief working with Tom Marble. The second man was Marble himself and he was very dead.

A few minutes later, Betty whipped the buggy into the ranch yard and then slewed it around to a shuddering halt.

"Marshal!" she cried, a rifle pressed to her cheek and shoulder. "Is that you?"

"It is," Longarm assured her.

"Thank heavens!" she cried, jumping down and giving him a big hug.

Longarm held her tight for a few moments, and then he went inside to find a lantern. While rummaging about

181

in the cabin he heard Betty wail, and he hurried back outside with the lantern still unlit.

"What is it!"

"He's *dead*!" she cried. "Jim is dead!"

It was true. The Assassin had bled to death, just as Longarm had feared. The best that could be hoped for was that the mysterious Jim Smith had at least enjoyed the satisfaction of knowing the last of the Marble Gang was also dead and justice had finally been served.

"Betty," Longarm said, again drawing the grieving woman close, "I'm sorry, but maybe it all worked out for the best."

"How can you *say* that!"

"Because," Longarm softly answered, "I know he would have never been able to stop judging and killing those he thought deserved to die."

Betty pulled away in the moonlight and glared up at him. "You know this because, except for the badge, he was like *you*!"

Longarm figured that she was a mite closer to the mark than he cared to admit, so he nodded, allowing Betty to rush back into his arms and have a good cleansing cry.

Watch for

LONGARM AND THE WHISKEY WOMAN

217th novel in the bold LONGARM series
from Jove

Coming in January!

If you enjoyed this book, subscribe now and get...

TWO FREE

A $7.00 VALUE—

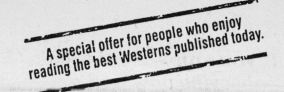